Please return/renew this item
by the last date shown.
Books may also be renewed by
phone and Internet
Telford and Wrekin Libraries

CITIES WITHOUT PALMS

TAREK ELTAYEB

TRANSLATED BY
KAREEM JAMES PALMER ZAID

ARABIA BOOKS

LONDON

First published in Great Britain in 2009 by
Arabia Books
70 Cadogan Place
London SW1X 9AH
www.arabia-books.co.uk

This edition published by arrangement with
The American University in Cairo Press
113 Sharia Kasr el Aini, Cairo, Egypt
420 Fifth Avenue, New York, NY 10018
www.aucpress.com

ISBN 978-1-906697-12-9

Printed in England by J. F. Print Ltd., Sparkford, Somerset
Cover design: Arabia Books
Cover image: Magnum

For my mother Zeinab and my father Eltayeb

From the Village

Sitting on a rock in front of our mud-brick house, I hold a dry stick in my hand. My many competing thoughts flow into one end of it, while its other end sketches strange lines and letters in the earth. If there is any meaning in these forms, it is unintended, for I am lost in my sad thoughts.

I press the stick down into the cracked, barren earth in anger and disgust. The violence and bitterness inside of me rises to my throat: I spit on the ground, cursing this merciless poverty and desolation. Then I sigh, remembering my father and what he did to us, and spit once more. I hate that man, and I am sure he hates me and my mother, and my two younger sisters as well. Why else would he marry another woman and abandon us like that? We never heard anything from him again, though we were once told that he was selling soda at a souk in Khartoum, and once that he was working on the railroad at Wadi Halfa, and another time that he had gone to Egypt and was working as a waiter in a coffeehouse.

Curse this life. Why did he abandon us? If he was incapable of supporting a family, why did he get married in the first place?

I increase the pressure on the dried-out stick, breaking it repeatedly until my fingertips are touching the clefts in the ground. I look at these cracks that crisscross the earth like a cobweb and, using my feet, try to cover them up with dirt. But what can two small feet do for an entire village? The desert keeps growing, and sorrow, not rain, is all that comes to us. Drought and disease, agony and death: we are the dying, the living dead. A dusty wind blows in, so I close my eyes for a few moments, then open them to see my black feet covered in dead dust, dust that wants to swallow me alive just as it swallowed hundreds of people from our village, and many from the neighboring villages too. I want to cry, but I cannot. I try to force a single teardrop from my eye, but it refuses to fall, as if I too have become utterly dry and desolate, like our village. I curse my father once again. Before he left, he taught me that weeping was for women and that a man must never cry, no matter what the circumstances. Curse your wisdom, you coward. I wish you had kept it to yourself.

One of the palm fronds that form the roof of our poor house flies off and falls to the ground. I pick it up between my fingertips. I think and spit, then think some more. I twist the frond around the tip of my ring finger and press down on it. I feel nothing, even as its sharp tip cuts into my skin. I press my finger into the dirt, just as we did when we were children. Whenever one of us hurt our foot or hand while playing, we simply pressed the wound into the earth until the bleeding stopped, and then we continued with our game.

I watch the children playing. Where are the ones today that resemble my childhood friends? I see only the specters of children, small ghosts dancing before me. Hunger has worn them down; bones protrude from their emaciated bodies; mangy, dust-colored skin covers their ribs and knees. Some of them are running around. Some of them are yelling. And others, too thin and weak to move, sit on the ground and take part in the game from a distance by screaming, only by screaming. This is a new game with which I am not familiar. When one of the children sees the others move away from him, he knows that they do not want him to join in the game, not even by shouting. This causes him to yell even more, and to keep yelling until his voice cracks. He weeps hoarsely until his mother comes and suckles him from breasts that resemble my mother's empty purse. I look at the child, and his two large, expectant eyes seem to cover his entire face. One of his hands clutches his mother's breast and the other her braids, and all the while flies gather around his eyes and pustules; they crowd around the wounds of his rickety body. Then they move to his mouth, hoping to share in his mother's milk; but nothing is there, so they return to assailing his emaciated body, falling upon its every wound—if there is no milk, then let there be blood.

Even if the entire village were to die, the flies would still remain. During the day they suck the children's blood, retreating only at night, when the mosquitoes come to claim their share. Their share of the remaining blood.

I used to play by some of the palm trees when I was young. I would carry a tin cup in one hand and a thick nylon bag in the other. This bag contained quite a few small stones and pebbles that I would throw into the heights of the palms, thereby obtaining some of the green dates that had not yet ripened. I would gobble up most of them, and bring the rest to a friend of mine. He used to let me play with him for an hour or so if I gave him some. Yet he was an unkind child, and only let me play with him until he had finished eating the dates, at which point he always ended the game. So then I would subserviently return to the palms and throw stones until my tiny arms were numb. At dusk I would head back home, carrying the green dates with me so I could give them to him the next day. But after a few minutes I would begin eating the dates. "What does it matter?" I would say to myself. "I'll get some more dates tomorrow, so I might as well have my fill now."

I used to see a boundless green world before me. It might not have been as vast as I had imagined, yet at least there was greenery, at least there was life. Then, one day, those hated insects advanced upon us and sucked the life out of all that was green. They turned everything into a single color, the color of that nothingness that bears ruin and death. Even the clouds that sometimes used to crawl above our village, the clouds that shielded it from the heat or brought it rain— even they stopped visiting us. If they appear at all now it is only from a frustrating distance, never close enough to protect us from the heat, but always far enough to make a quick and cruel escape.

I remember when a friend of my father once brought me a toy car so that I could play like the other children. My father berated me for the gift. "He should learn something useful!" he remarked to his friend. And so he left me with Sheikh Ali al-Faki. It was said that the sheikh had studied at al-Azhar University in Cairo. In spite of his youth, he enjoyed great respect in our village, where his word was like law. I had heard from others, though, that he had not actually studied at al-Azhar, but rather that he had spent those two years in Egypt trying his luck in business, and that he had only returned to the village after his ventures failed. In any case, he is the only one from our village who has ever traveled anywhere, not only to the city but outside the country; there is no doubt that he is more knowledgeable than the rest us, and that he deserves our respect. In our insignificance, we have become accustomed to respecting newcomers from afar.

I remember how Sheikh al-Faki used to rebuke me for skipping prayers so often. My father would then menacingly bear down on me, telling the sheikh, "Beat him. Do what you like with him. I want him to be a good son." He used to go to the mosque with Sheikh al-Faki, yet when he came home he had only insults for the man. "He's a sinner disguised as a sheikh," he would say. Then he would sit down and chew his tobacco, spitting on every clean spot of ground that he could find. No, my father only had respect for the sheikh when he was in his presence. At those times I always heard him say, "You're our sheikh and our scholar, may God bless you!" Then, for no reason at all, he would tremble in anger and scream at me to bring tea from the house to where they were sitting outside. To this day I do not know why he always had to yell at me whenever he wanted tea. I was very young then, yet I still felt as if I was taking Sheikh al-Faki's place as the recipient of this abuse. And as my father's insults increased, so did my hatred for the sheikh.

Once, when Sheikh al-Faki was teaching me the ablutions to be performed before prayer, he caught me laughing with the others, then saw a spot on my heel untouched by water. He grew angry and swore at me, "Do it right, you ass!" I used to go to prayer and stand in the back with the other children. Yet when everyone else bowed and touched their foreheads to the ground, I would simply sit and watch them. Though I never had the faintest idea why, this scene often sent a wave of laughter over me. I would try to hold it back, but it would still come out, muffled yet sharp like the cries of an ape. Sheikh al-Faki would call me once he had ended the prayer, for he knew my laugh well and, armed with my father's order to teach me discipline, he would bring out the cane. The lashes burned my body, each one trying to make me repent and come to my senses. In the evening, the sheikh would relate all of this to my father, who in turn would seize the opportunity to beat me, the hard blows from his cane raining down upon my head. My father would strike me even more harshly than usual in the presence of the sheikh, as if to prove to him that he was punishing me as best he could; or perhaps he imagined that I was Sheikh Ali al-Faki as he beat me. My mother was the only one who ever came to my rescue. She would run to me in concern and place herself between me and my devil of a father, saying, "Can't you show the boy some mercy? Don't you see he's weak? And you, Sheikh Ali, you only ever visit us to complain about my son. Aren't there any other children in the village?"

My father would spring at me once again, cursing my mother and warning her not to get involved. "The sheikh's instructions are for the boy's own good," he would say, "and we should follow his advice." Then he would chide her for interfering, and she would bring them two cups of tea.

The thing I hated most in my small world was the sight of Sheikh Ali al-Faki walking about the village. He used to slither through it like a serpent, bringing venom to the families, encouraging parents to torment their children.

He took pleasure in his sadistic spirit. He enjoyed seeing the pain of others, especially children. Whenever I saw him approaching our house, I knew that he was bringing disaster, the kind whose cane would fall upon my skull. And so I always ran off to the distant graveyard to hide. I often met other vagrant children along the way, and from them I learned to smoke, sniff gasoline, and wage war on the children of the small neighboring villages by throwing pebbles and stones at them. Then I would keep going until I reached the graves, where I would sit alone for the rest of the day, singing to myself.

I do not know how old I am now—there are no birth records in our village. I think that I am about nineteen or twenty. The years passed quickly, and my only memories are of a mostly happy childhood. Yes, happy. Any childhood, even one marked by misery, contains something of happiness; for the life of a child is a life without responsibilities, a life that is vast and free, limitless. Well, it may not have been entirely free, but a few hours of freedom each day were enough to keep me satisfied.

I have two younger sisters: one of them is six years old, and the other four. The younger one suffers from stomach pain; she is all skin and bones, just like the rest of the village's new generation. My other sister suffers from chronic inflammation of her eyes; every now and again my mother takes her to Sheikha Salma to get something to rub in them. As for my mother, her life has been harsh. She is gaunt and wasted now, not least because of the many unborn children she lost between me and my sisters.

Whenever I think about this life, about all its sickness and poverty, I feel sorrow and pain, and also bitterness, for our current situation is erasing the few sweet memories we have and forcing us to live like beetles—we crawl slowly across the sands, awaiting our fate.

Enough of these memories. I feel the pressure of responsibilities, responsibilities I never knew before. They bear down on my chest and bring a bitter taste to my mouth, so bitter I cannot even swallow. And so I spit, while my mind spins in the painful vortex that is the future.

The Wad al-Nur family left a week ago to their relatives in Omdurman. They were so close, so dear to us, particularly after my father's departure. My mother used to help them with the cooking and cleaning, and we were always welcome to eat with them whenever we liked. And despite there not being enough food for all our tiny mouths, not one of them ever grumbled about our life together; they only ever complained about how my father had treated us. We ourselves have no relatives that I know of. I had heard from my father—when he was still with us—that he had a relative who worked in the city, and that the cousin of his aunt's sister was one of the richest businessmen in Port Sudan. But I never saw either of them. I only saw this large and loving family, the Wad al-Nur family, which consisted of Abd al-Malik, the father, and al-Batul, the mother, and her sister Miriam, and four sons and three daughters, all of whom lived together in a house larger than ours, a house with a big radio.

The Wad al-Nurs were my family, after my mother. They gave me more love and affection than anyone else. I cried dryly on the day of their departure—not a single teardrop fell from my eyes. As for my mother, she too wept, and remained shut up in her room until Miriam, al-Batul, and her husband came to say goodbye, leaving some money under my mother's pillow.

Leaning on the remains of a large, half-broken jar near the door of the house, I watched everyone cry. I could not bear their goodbyes, so I fled to the graves. I stayed there until sunset, and when I finally returned hoping to see them and say goodbye, my mother said, "Where were you all day? They waited over two hours to say goodbye to you. But then they realized that it was the pain of seeing them leave that was keeping you away, so they left you their greetings; and Abd al-Malik left you his watch as a present for you to remember him by." I snatched the watch from my mother and looked at it. I hated myself for not having said goodbye to him and his children—my only childhood friends—before their departure. I do not know if I will ever see him again. Abd al-Malik had brought me up with his own two hands ever since my father left us almost five years ago, while my mother was still pregnant with my youngest sister Halima. He was a good father to me.

A week has gone by, yet I am still caught in that moment when the Wad al-Nur family left Wad al-Nar, this village whose *nar*—its fire—consumes its people day after day. I remember how I used to go to the store each morning to buy some flour or sugar or tea. When I returned home, my mother would bake a few pieces of bread while I sat behind her, following her and my little sister Halima with my eyes. Halima would put on her gloves beside my mother and sink her fingers playfully in the dough. Sometimes my mother would laugh at this, but sometimes she would scold Halima for getting carried away with her game. Then Halima would eagerly wait for the bread to bake. She always tried to push an entire piece into her small mouth in one go, so I would pick her up and, laughing with her, put a few small bites in her mouth, which she always gobbled up in the blink of an eye. I would give her another piece, and then another, until she started to play with the bread rather than eat it. Then I would take the piece from her and eat it myself, and my mother would bring some more for me and my sister Karima. "Don't you want to eat something?" I always asked my mother. And she always replied, "No, I'm not hungry now. I'll eat later." I knew she had not eaten anything since the morning. I knew she was going hungry to make sure her children had enough, so I would implore her to eat something. She always refused, but I used to keep at it until she reluctantly ate a bit.

After wandering through these thoughts a long while, I go into the house and return with a cup of tea that I set down beside me. I grab another stick and poke it into the ground, spitting and thinking. At this moment, before I have finished breaking the stick, the thought of leaving for the city occurs to me. I could go there and work, help support my mother and two sisters. If it is not possible for all of us to leave this ruined village, then I will go by myself. I can send money to my mother to help her get by, until I am able to take her and my sisters someplace else, somewhere that still has life.

In the distance I can see Sheikh Ali al-Faki making the rounds with his usual zeal. He inspects the village every afternoon, equitably doling out punishment among its children. My sisters were spared, for girls do not attend the sheikh's lessons. I no longer hate him as I did when I was younger, yet I still dislike how harshly he deals with the children of our village. They are so poor and miserable. These children have no fancy games, they have nothing to keep them occupied, nor do they have the schools of the cities that I hear about. Rather, most of them just play in the sand, naked as the day they were born. This is the new generation, a generation molded by the pain of poverty and famine. Day after day, their bodies fill with dirt. New diseases creep into them with each passing hour. Death advances on them like a serpent on an injured bird, a bird that long ago lost the gift of flight. Our village has changed. I was proud of it when I was younger. It used to be green. And I used to be happy among its palms. Now it has become a graveyard, a gaping tomb that swallows its victims and slowly digests them.

Seeing all of this, I hate for any other burdens to weigh down on the village, whether from Sheikh al-Faki or anyone else. We need medicine as much as we need food, and we need food more than knowledge. Hunger has spread from our stomachs to our minds, and now our heads are filled with it—how can he expect us to learn like this? I fear for the children of my small village, this village that I love so dearly. I would not have it fall into oblivion. I want to die here; I want be buried in that graveyard where I so often hid from the punishment of my father. I feel closer to the graves than I do to him; I harbor a certain love for them that I never bore for my father, for they protected me from his beatings. I used to sit among them for hours, singing. I was the sole composer of those songs, the lone conductor, and their only audience.

I used to listen to stories about jinn and demons that were said to live in the graveyard, yet I was never scared of them. I always felt safe among the graves. No fear could reach me in that place.

I see Sheikh al-Faki approaching. He greets me, "How are you today Hamza?"

"How well can one be in our village?"

As he draws near his eyes scour the ground in search of a rug, and I realize he wants to chat and drink a cup of tea, as usual. I point to a sheepskin that my father used to pray on in front of the house whenever he wanted to demonstrate his piety to the village. Sheikh al-Faki takes off his sandals and sits down cross-legged on the rug, then asks—as always—the hated question, "Haven't you heard anything about your father?"

"I don't want to hear anything about him."

"He's still your father, and children are obliged to respect their fathers."

"Tell me, Sheikh Ali, who bears the obligations here? Shouldn't the father first fulfill his own? Listen to me, sheikh: I don't want to talk about this with you." Then I call out, "Karima!"

Karima emerges from the house and I ask her to bring us two cups of tea, then turn to the sheikh. "What are your thoughts on traveling?" I ask.

"Where to? I have so many responsibilities here: education, and prayer, and . . . ."

I interrupt him, "I don't mean for you to travel. I'm the one who would leave."

"You?" he says incredulously. "Where would you go?"

"God's kingdom is vast, and you know I'm the only one who can help my mother and sisters now. You know there's no hope for us in this village." I turn away from him and spit on the ground.

Sheikh al-Faki stares at me, astonished by my words, but does not make a sound. I continue, "I'll go to the city and try to find work there, and all I'm asking of you is to look after my mother and sisters while I'm gone, to protect them until I return. I'll send them whatever money I make. And you can write me to let me know how they're doing."

As I speak these words, I hold another stick in my hand and poke it into the ground, while Sheikh al-Faki produces a pack of tobacco and begins to chew. We both spit, though for different reasons: he from pleasure and I from bitterness. And when Karima brings us our tea, he asks her if there is enough sugar in it, to which she replies, "Yes, five spoons, just like always."

The sheikh looks at me again. "What do you think of my plan?" I ask.

"Trust in God, and I'll do all that I can for you. And may God help us."

Then he starts to tell me about his glory days, when he studied at al-Azhar in Cairo. He has told me this story so often that I have it committed to memory, so I pay no attention to him, but instead think about my impending journey, wondering where I will go and how long it will last. Is this a mistake? Should I stay? But what would I do here if I stayed? Try to take my family someplace else? And where, where in all this arid land could we possibly take root again? Sheikh al-Faki is still talking, and I am still breaking sticks in the ground. I think and spit, and once he notices that I am not listening and that there is no point in talking to me right now, he clears his throat to leave. Before he goes, I say, "Sheikh al-Faki, don't forget: They're in your care."

"I'll do what I can, and may God be merciful."

I pour the rest of his tea onto the dried earth and roll up the sheepskin. Carrying the rug under my arm, I pick up the two cups and walk into the house.

Inside the house, I find my mother singing to Halima and putting her in a big basin to bathe her. Halima laughs happily until some soap gets in her eyes, whereupon she starts screaming and squirming about, desperately trying to escape from the basin. My mom grabs her head and holds her fast, evoking even more fearful screams from my sister. I laugh and stroll through the house, my hands on my waist, thinking about the future of my two poor sisters. My mother asks Karima to get Halima's clothes—the bath is over. Halima looks at me and laughs, for the crisis has ended well. I pick her up, kiss her, and carry her outside. I tell her some made-up stories as I walk, and at first she listens with interest. But once she realizes that I am simply repeating tales I have already told her, she begins to hit me with her two tiny hands and to kick me with her two small feet, trying to escape to the ground, where she has caught sight of a group of children building pyramids in the sand. I try to hold onto her, but as usual she is faster and more persistent than I am. She escapes and takes up her place on the ground among the playing children. I threaten her but she pays no heed, so I go back to the house. When my mother sees me alone, she asks, "Where's Halima?"

"Playing with the other children."

"After her bath?"

"What's new about that?"

I call to my mother and tell her that I have made up my mind about something, and briefly explain my plan to leave. She sadly bows her head and silently looks at the ground for a while—I think she is going to cry. I manage to remain calm as I walk quickly outside, then remind her that I intend to leave tomorrow morning, while the sun is still low in the sky.

I visit my silent city: I go to the graves to bid them farewell. I am not sure how long I stay there. For once, I do not sing. I simply sit there, lost in my memories.

Suddenly I realize that I am leaving tomorrow. I think less about the road ahead or about what will become of me than I do about leaving my mother and two young sisters alone in the village.

Perched on top of a palm tree, a crow caws loudly and startles me. The palm has lost all its fronds—I cannot bear to watch it die like this. It was the only palm that survived near the graves. It was *my* palm tree, I was its sole keeper. The children never approached it, for the many tales of jinn and demons kept them away from the graveyard; and so I could always have as many of its green dates as I wanted. We have shared so many memories, the palm and I, and now it is dying, silently dying while the crow caws on its barren summit, announcing its dominion over the palm's ruined kingdom.

I hastily say goodbye to my mother the following morning. Halima springs upon me. I carry her on my shoulders, letting her feet dangle in front of my chest. She holds firmly onto my matted hair, as she always does. Karima stands beside me, for she knows that I will be gone for some time. She says, "I want to go with you Hamza."

"I'll come back soon. As soon as I can."

I direct this reply at my mother. She is clearly all choked up, but she says nothing, maintaining a sad and painful silence. I know she is holding back her tears—she does not want to cause me any pain. I have no idea how she manages to control herself. All that I know is that my mother, ever since my father left us years ago, has always been strong and patient, has always put on a bold face for the sake of us children. And now it is my turn to take action. Halima once more tugs at my hair, "Let's go!" she says.

"Where to, you little monster? Get down now, get down— I've got to get going."

She laughs, not seeming to understand me, "Let's go play!" she says.

I peel her off my shoulders and put her down, then grab hold of her feet and playfully tackle her just like I always do. "I'm going to eat you!" I yell, and she laughs and kicks her feet in the air, making contact with my shoulder. I cry out feigning pain, then pretend to be dead. She laughs again, and I go after her once more. We play a little while longer, until I am all worn out. Halima, however, remains full of energy.

I give my mother a long hug, and kiss her and my two sisters. My mother removes an amulet from around her neck. She inherited it from her mother when she gave birth to me and has always had it with her, for she believes it protects her from evil. She puts it around my neck and asks me to keep it safe, telling me it will ward off disaster and protect me from the jinn and demons, from all that is wicked in this world. My fingertips graze its surface. My mother's words put me at ease, for I really do believe them. Then I pick up the small bag made of palm fronds that my mother had hastily prepared for me and walk out the door of our house.

A wind kicks up dust into my eyes, filling them with tears. I look behind me and see Halima standing by my mother, hitting her violently on the thigh and screaming because she wants to come with me. My mother holds onto one of her hands so she cannot escape and run after me. I walk with my neck craned backward, watching the three of them as they wave goodbye. The wind kicks up again. I rub the dust and tears from my eyes.

I pass by Sheikh al-Faki's house. He usually pays me no heed, but this time he raises his hands in greeting. I remind him about my mother and sisters, saying, "I'll write you whenever I can—make sure you write back to tell me how they are." He gives me a document that bears my name and some other personal information, as well as several inscriptions and signatures, and tells me that this is my identity card, and that I should always carry it with me in the city. I fold it up and put it in a pouch that contains a little money and that I have tied around my waist. I have not forgotten the watch either. I put it on my wrist, even though I have some difficulty telling the time with it.

I put a few miles between myself and my small village; I look at the watch and feel the amulet; and the more I walk, the more my village melts away behind me, until it disappears completely. There is no road here, nor are there any landmarks, and were it not for the knowledge from my days of youth—those days when I waged war with pebbles and stones—I would not have known the invisible paths that lead through this desert. I see a dead donkey, a foul smell emanating from it. I spit on the ground and quicken my pace, impatient to arrive at the next village. I catch sight of some moving figures and also some fixed structures in the distance, and I know that it is the village. The last time I came here was many years ago, when the people from all the nearby villages came out to watch a documentary film that someone from the capital had brought to show us. We were so happy that day, happy watching a wall on which people were moving and talking. I remember the lovely clothes they were wearing, and how the color of their skin took on so many different shades between black and white. The film was about one of the development projects in the country, about plans to set up some new dams and farms—plans that have yet to be realized.

All of this goes through my mind as I enter the village once again. It seems as if this place too has taken a turn for the worse. It is still bigger than our village, but no better off. The faces are the same as the ones in our village; the poverty is the same; and the cracked, thirsty earth is just as devoid of plants or crops. I see the same waiting, the same subdued, dejected eyes on the faces of the old. I see the same destitution, the same fear in the eyes of the young. I hear the same cries from the children. There is nothing new here.

I ask the people of the village about the van that is supposed to travel to the railway, and they tell me that it is at the other end of the village. It makes the trip to the railway once every week, and today is the day it leaves, as Sheikh al-Faki had said. I go find the owner, and see him peering under the open hood of his vehicle, trying to fix the motor. I tell him that I will be traveling with him to the railway. He looks me over from top to bottom without saying a word. I see a few people sitting on the ground by the van, waiting to get started.

Once the engine is running, the driver stands up and collects the fare from the passengers, then we all get in. Their faces are lifeless—some of them stare blankly out the windows into space, while others talk and laugh in voices as shrill as the cracking of whips.

I wearily lean my back in a corner of the van while the air begins to heat up. Dust kicks up and covers our faces—we look like we have come straight from the grave. I rest my head and try to sleep, while my mind wanders back to my mother and sisters, back to Wad al-Nar.

I wake up suddenly. The engine churns loudly as the van bounces along the sand like a startled rabbit, swaying like a ship on a rocky sea. I hear the din of wood grating against iron and expect the whole thing to break down at any moment. The van stops a little while later, stuck in the sand, its tires frantically spinning in place and stubbornly refusing to move forward. The tires dig themselves into the sand while the driver tries to move on: the longer he tries, the deeper we sink. He curses the car and the road; he curses man and jinn and devils. We get out to help him, and pull out the long metal sheets that we had been sitting on. We place them under the tires, positioning and repositioning them until the wheels finally move forward, then we all jump in again.

The passengers begin to get more familiar with each other once the crisis is over. The man sitting beside me offers me a cigarette, which I gratefully accept, and we strike up a conversation typical of this sort of situation: What's your name, where are you from, where are you going? I discover that the man knows more about the city than he does about my small village, one so close to his own.

Our conversation is interrupted by the driver getting out and once more cursing and swearing. We follow him out the car to find out what is happening, but we see nothing at all—only a vast and featureless desert that stretches as far as the eye can see in every direction. We realize that the driver has gotten lost—he has been drinking the whole time. Everyone starts cursing in turn, and it begins to look like no one is sure of the way, but then one of the passengers says he thinks he can still direct us to the railroad. He takes a seat beside the driver to better see the way.

The second crisis passes. We all jump back into the vehicle, which resumes its journey through the desert, bouncing so violently now that I can almost feel my bones snapping beneath my skin. Suddenly, the driver's voice rises up out of the tumult, "The railway!" We all get out, and I quickly ask about the train heading to the capital—the others tell me that it is the grey train on the second track. Before boarding the train, I find a large clay jar filled with warm water and drink from it until I quench my thirst. Then I pour a cup over my head, and the dust clinging to my neck and face turns to mud, but I pay no heed. I run for the train, which is already beginning to drag itself toward the city.

I sit down in one of the cars on a long wooden bench near the window. When I try to close the window to stop the incoming dust, I realize it has no glass. I find my bag of food and pull out a cold piece of bread. I chew it while my eyes explore the other passengers, some of them sitting upright and others sleeping, their loud snores filling the air and mixing with the violent clatter of the train. Whenever the train stops somewhere for a few minutes, I look curiously at the new passengers. And whenever it stops for longer than a few minutes, I look around nervously, wondering whether this vehicle too has lost its way.

As we travel onward, the signs of life steadily increase—I see ever more greenery and ever more people, people whose clothes become cleaner and lovelier with each passing mile. I wander in my thoughts back to Wad al-Nar and touch my mother's amulet, sensing that it will protect me from this vast and unfamiliar world. I spit out the window. Then I lie down on the long wooden bench and sleep for a while, until an old man looking for a place to sit wakes me up. I make room for him beside me—he falls asleep a couple minutes later, making a pillow of my shoulder.

I rest my head on the windowsill and look out the train, but I do not see a thing. Darkness has set in, both inside and out, and as the faint rays of a single lamp at the far end of the car finally die out, slumber prevails over the few remaining passengers that have stayed awake, while the clatter of the train continues. My fingers unconsciously move across my new watch, and I think of Abd al-Malik, wondering if I will ever see him in the city. Then I touch the amulet and think of my mother and sisters: When will I come back to them? I ask myself.

I sleep the rest of the way, oblivious of just how many hours go by, for the long journey—and my curiosity—has left me exhausted.

The morning comes quickly. All sorts of voices—tender and harsh, pleasant and hideous—rise and fall in the air. Everyone begins to gather up their belongings, readying themselves to get off the train. I peer out the window and think: This must be the city; this is how the people describe it in their stories.

To the City

I get off the train with the others, feeling my way forward like someone walking in the dark. Hands flail against me, feet kick out at me, the swinging suitcases slam into my back and elbows—everything is so quick, chaotic. I turn this way and that, trying to take it all in, like a child lost in the crowd.

The voice of an old man carrying several bags and boxes catches my attention—he addresses me almost angrily, telling me to help him carry his load. I pick up a few of his bags and walk with him until we emerge onto a large plaza. "Put the bags here my boy, and thank you," he says.

I continue on my way, my ears filled with an intense din whose like I have never heard before. Cars of all makes and colors fly by at astonishing speeds—I have only ever rarely seen cars in my life, and never so many of them. The people too are different. They walk so quickly here; they seem to leap through the lines of speeding cars. I hear their voices all around me, their greetings, their conversations, their laughter, all of it blending into the roaring engines and honking horns. I see men wearing clean white robes, their heads wrapped in white turbans. I see women in bright silk dresses walking behind them. And I see others dressed very differently, men and women whose clothes remind me of stories I had heard about the English during the occupation.

I am a bit thirsty, so I look around for a water jar but fail to find one. Instead I find a store selling colorful juices at different prices. I choose the cheapest one and order a cup of it, but it fails to quench my thirst. I order another, and then another. It tastes strange and wonderful, and at this very moment I think of my mother and my two sisters, wishing that they could enjoy this delicious drink with me.

I slowly continue on my way, looking about in all directions, my eyes following the people's movements. And whenever someone stops and stares at me, I simply say hello, for it is our custom in the village to greet passersby. Yet no one in this wondrous city takes any interest in a stranger. Many of the people walk in groups, and sometimes some of them stop to greet an acquaintance, yet everything here is different from the ways of my village. Even the stores are different. They are grouped together here, and you often find four or more lined up one after the other, all of them selling the same things.

I try to cross the street, but the cars rushing by in all directions force me back to the sidewalk. So I keep walking along my side of the road until I find a way to get across— I would rather cross a river than this horrific street. Suddenly, a delicious smell reaches my nose and drags it forward until I find myself standing at the door of a restaurant, my mouth watering. I see groups of people eating inside, and there is a steady flow of customers both into and out of the place. I marvel at the sight of people eating outside their homes. The stories I had heard in the village make it easier for me to understand many of these strange new things, but that does not lessen my amazement. I look at the delectable food from behind the windowpane. Then I look at the prices: they are higher than I had expected. My hand reaches into my bag and touches the bread I had brought with me, which has become cold and stale by now. I raise my eyes once again, this time ignoring the prices and looking only at the food, and my mouth waters even more.

I eat like someone who has just emerged from the desert, then loathingly pay the bill. The little money I have with me will not permit any more meals of this sort.

God! What will I do in this enormous city? I feel lost. I feel as if I were in the middle of a vast and boundless sea: everyone must swim here, myself included, for I will sink to the bottom if I do not. I decide to introduce myself in some of the shops and businesses that I have seen—perhaps I can find work in one of them. I retrace my steps and present myself to all the various store owners as if my very person were a product to be sold. Some of them look at me as though they do not hear a word I say; others turn their faces away from me or motion for me to leave; and still others are polite and apologize for not being able to offer me any work.

Where can I find work? I ask myself. I need to find something, anything. Otherwise I will not survive, nor will those I left behind in the village.

When I finally succeed in crossing the street, the hope of finding a job once again takes hold of me. Yet whether calmly or rudely, whether indifferently or with a certain degree of surprise, the shopkeepers all give me the same answer. I continue through the city, bewildered but with eyes on the prowl, scouting for work while being bombarded by so many new and unfamiliar scenes. Overwhelmed by it all, I sometimes stop suddenly in the middle of the sidewalk, causing other people to crash into me. The adults often swear at me, while the children usually just look at me in bewilderment.

The long and hopeless walk through the city has left me out of breath. It is incredibly hot, so much so that the pavement has heated up my sandals, which are now stinging the soles of my feet. I move to the shade to escape this torment, leaning on the side of a store and considering my next move.

Without warning, a tall young man suddenly appears in front of me. His curly, unkempt hair has a dark red hue to it. His old, dirty clothes are in the style of the English, and there is a certain crafty air about him. He is holding a pack of cigarettes in his hand and smoking in long, drawn-out drags, exhaling the smoke simultaneously through both his mouth and nose.

He addresses me, "How are you, my friend?"

"Not that well, as you can see. I'm exhausted—this heat is killing me."

"I can tell from your accent that you're not from the city."

"No, I'm not. I'm from a village called Wad al-Nar, hundreds of miles from here."

He closes his eyes and repeats what he has just heard, as if trying to remember something, "Wad al-Nar . . . Wad al-Nar. . . . What family are you from?"

"You don't even know the name of my village, so how would you know the name of my family?"

He laughs and says, "You're a light-hearted one, son of Nar!"

"My name's Hamza."

"Your name's not important. Tell me who you're looking for here."

"I don't know a soul in this city. I came here to look for work."

He looks at me in disbelief, as if I were crazy, "And what sort of work are you looking for?"

"Any work. I need money, and my family needs it too. We've been reduced to poverty, and I had no choice but to leave and look for any work that I could find. I thought that since the city is so large, there might be a chance of finding something here."

"I see. And what can you do?"

This time I look at him with a mixture of supplication and mistrust. Is he trying to provoke me with this question? Either he is unemployed himself and looking for entertainment, or is sincere and truly interested in finding work for me. With this thought in my mind, I reply, "I can do any job I'm given. Do you know of something?"

"Let me think a bit. For the moment, don't worry about anything. Get up and I'll take you to some friends of mine."

I stand up wearily and, caught between joy and doubt, begin another long walk through the city. We go through neighborhood after neighborhood, and pass street after street, and all the while I keep looking behind me to try to remember the way. Is this all a trick? Each neighborhood resembles the other, and the shops all seem the same, as if we were walking in circles. We finally arrive at an old house with a large door of rusted iron. He gives the door a couple of clear and patterned knocks—a young man opens it, groggy from sleep. He lets us in and greets me as if he knows who I am. I take a quick look around me—as the stranger in a strange place is wont to do—and when I turn back the man is gone. He has disappeared without a trace.

I address my new friend, "What work will I be doing?"

"Relax," he replies. "Rest a while from your journey. In any case, our work begins at night. I'll tell you all about it after you've had a rest."

His words reassure me, though I still cannot shake the doubt and uncertainty from my thoughts. As I sit down on a carpet, a wave of exhaustion washes over me. I find myself lying on my elbows, then on my side, and finally I fall into oblivion. I sleep like a dead man, forsaking both the world and its dreams.

I wake up to the sound of a heated discussion. I hear five different voices—they are clearly talking about me. I pretend to be asleep so I can figure out what is happening. I realize that a couple of them want me to stay, but that the others are against the idea. One of them speaks out very harshly, each sentence of his containing a few choice vulgarities to express just what he thinks of my being here. He reminds my friend of the idiot he brought in last month and who got caught, while the rest of them barely managed to escape into the safety of the night.

I get up to greet the group, but the one who was speaking gives me such an evil look that I stop in my tracks. I look at this giant in terror. The whites of his eyes are tinged with yellow and red; they seem to be popping out of their sockets. His teeth are all black, and there is a deep scar above his left eyebrow, which adds to the harshness of his features. He is wearing a dirty white robe that reaches slightly below his knees, as well as a large gold watch on his right arm, and a black bracelet made of fine leather on his left one. When I finally manage to get close enough to shake everyone's hands, I catch a whiff of a very familiar smell emanating from the giant's body: gasoline. Before extending his hand to me, he coarsely asks, "What's your name?"

"Hamza."

"Where are you from?"

"The village of Wad al-Nar," I say in an ever-diminishing voice. "I doubt you've heard of it."

My strange accent seems to convince him that I'm telling the truth. He slowly looks me over. "Are you ready to work with us tonight?" he asks.

I do not think to ask about where or how. I take a deep breath, like a prisoner who has just been granted a pardon, and quickly reply, "Yes. Yes, I'm ready."

"Alright then. Al-Khattaf will explain everything to you, and I expect you to do a good job—I won't tolerate any ignorance or stupidity, do you understand?"

"Of course I do. Of course. You'll see how well I work."

He does not say another word. I have no idea what they are keeping from me, but it seems as if tonight's work may not be entirely legal.

Thinking about my family and the village, I touch the amulet and whisper to myself: Today I found a place to stay, and I'll start working soon enough, so just put off your curiosity until tonight.

Al-Khattaf—'the thief'—sits beside me. It was he who met me in the street and brought me here. He keeps calling me "son of Nar," referring to my village, or perhaps because he simply likes the name. He begins explaining the work to me, "You know that there's a gasoline shortage in the city."

"Yes. Of course I know," I reply, though I know nothing at all about the shortage—I would rather lie than have him think I am an idiot.

"Great. After midnight we go to a large parking lot somewhere. 'The Whale' always picks the location—he's our boss, the man who was speaking to you a moment ago.

We go after the cars, each of us with his own specific task. One of us is in charge of opening the cars' fuel tanks, while another checks which ones have the most gasoline. I'm in charge of siphoning the gas into a container with a small tube; someone else keeps a lookout so we don't get caught; and the last two carry the siphoned gas to our own car, which is usually parked some distance away from the others. You will be one of the two people in charge of carrying the gas—do you think you can handle that?"

The thought of starting this work, the idea of getting myself involved with these people, frightens me. Yet the choice is clear: either I say yes and begin stealing with them; or I refuse and go back to the streets, and risk being forced to spend the night in the police station.

"Isn't there a chance we'll be arrested?" I ask him in a shaky voice.

"You seem afraid."

"I'm not afraid. I've just never stolen anything in my life."

He answers, coughing and laughing coarsely, "This isn't stealing, it's redistribution. The gas is poorly distributed during the day, and we fix this by redistributing it at night. Now, are you in or not?"

"Yes, I'm in," I say, clenching my teeth. "When do we start?"

"After midnight. You can go walk around a bit now. Or would you like to come to the movies?"

"Sure. I just don't have that much money."

"That doesn't matter. We have our own way of getting in."

I go to the cinema with them. We deftly jump over the back fence and sneak in, and all of us sit together to watch one of the American movies. I can't stop thinking about the job this evening (I see people kiss on the screen); I worry that someone will come and ask for my ticket (I see a gorgeous, scantily clad woman); in doubt, I look at my new friends who are watching the movie and laughing (the hero has a sword; he stabs the villain); I can no longer deny the fear I feel (one woman kills another with some poison). I watch the movie, but although I am astounded by what I see, my fear ruins the fun for me.

The second film begins, and my fear gradually slips away, allowing the movie to finally take hold of me. The music is wonderful, and the sight of horses running swiftly with gun-toting men on their backs delights me. They ride up mountains and descend into valleys. I hear them speak in a foreign language, and words appear at the bottom of the screen, but my poor reading skills are not quick enough to keep up with them. I barely manage to decipher two words before the entire line vanishes and a new one takes its place. I keep on trying until I realize that I am missing the entire movie. So I watch the rest of the movie without attempting to read the words at the bottom of the screen— the gestures and screaming of the characters are much easier for me to follow.

This film also ends with the hero bloodily defeating his adversary. He carries away the lovely woman on the only horse still alive and heads back home; then the music starts up again.

We leave the cinema through the main door. I see the attendants standing there and watching everyone leave. I look in the other direction as I go by, afraid they will realize I did not buy a ticket. Then we all go to a restaurant, where we are brought fuul—a dish made from stewed broad beans—with cheese. The others pay my bill for me after we have eaten, and I thank them.

The Whale and another one of our colleagues are waiting for us at the corner in an old Landrover. We jump into the car and head behind the giant souk of Omdurman, where many cars are parked, all crammed together. We circle the area twice to make sure no police are around, then the Whale parks in a dark spot behind a fence.

I pick up my container and walk to the appointed place. The work begins quickly and silently, a flurry of signals and whispers. I am terrified, and each time I hear the sound of a car—even one a mile away—my fear increases. One of my colleagues arrives with a small container filled with gasoline, which he then pours into another container. I keep one eye on the container and the other on the road, straining to see any movement, even that of a stray dog or a starving cat. "Don't be like that," my new colleague whispers. "Someone's watching the road right now, and if anything happens they'll let out a whistle and we'll calmly and quietly walk away, then meet the others back at the fence."

The job ends without incident and we head back to the derelict house. We had only been working an hour, yet it felt like an eternity. My fear has left me exhausted, and I fall into a deep sleep. I wake up the next morning in alarm. Who are these people? I ask myself. How did I get here? What am I doing here? What nightmare is this? A moment later the events of the previous day return to my mind. I look at the others sleeping around me and shut my eyes again. I try to fall asleep, to fall back into oblivion; but sleep doesn't come, and neither does oblivion.

The Whale went out—as I would later learn—to sell the stolen gasoline, and when he returns he distributes the money among us and tells me, "Today is Thursday. We don't work tonight because people stay out later and there's a greater chance of getting caught. So everyone can spend their evening as they please." One of my colleagues goes to the brothel; the second goes out to drink araq—a liquor made from aniseed; the third goes off to join some other friends; and I have no idea what the fourth one does. The last one, however, is crazy about movies, so I seize the opportunity to return to the cinema with him. We watch the same two films again, but it feels as if it is for the very first time, for there is no work at the end of the evening to wear on my nerves and spoil the movies. We go out to eat afterward, and this time I pay for my food out of my own pocket. Then we head back to the house.

Two weeks go by, and I have already managed to save up a fair amount of money from the robberies. I go to the post office and send some of the money to my mother in Wad al-Nar. I feel better after this, and impatiently wait for a reply to let me know that my mother received the money.

I continue working with the group for the next four months, during which time our schedule never changes. With the exception of our weekly night off on Thursdays, we always begin stealing gasoline after midnight. Watching movies becomes my pastime, and eating fuul with cheese becomes almost an addiction. I follow my friends' leads in everything and join them in all their activities, hoping to win their affection—this a way of forgetting, of losing myself, yet I fear that I may lose even this comforting form of loss. Sometimes I am able to enjoy myself, but other times I feel only danger and uncertainty. The lack of any word from my mother and sisters adds to my worries. I have sent them money four times and told them to write me at the nearest post office, where the letters can be held for me. I go by the post office every day, but to no avail. I immerse myself in the fleeting pleasures of this world to take my mind off my incessant worries.

As is so often the case in these matters, differences arise among the members of the crew, and this time they cannot be reconciled. Two of my colleagues quit, and I myself have grown tired of this dangerous work. I had hoped for something different in the city, and so I seize this opportunity to leave the group; no one cares that I am leaving, nor do they seem to care about what I will do next. And even though it means losing my one place of shelter, I take my leave of everything in that ruined house without any regrets.

The warm summer permits me to sleep in the open air, and I spend the next nine nights in public parks. When I wake up each morning, I feel as if mites—borne on the winds I endure as I sleep—have been gnawing on my bones all night. I spend the days looking for work, walking all across the city until my sandals are almost worn away. On the tenth day I run out of money. I head toward the spice market and ask every person with a shop, cart, or stand about work, but they have nothing for me, not even when I tell them that I am willing to work for room and board alone. I stamp around in rage, spitting and swearing and asking shopkeeper after shopkeeper, but it is hopeless. I fear for my mother and sisters. I rub my amulet and ask its forgiveness. I look at the watch on my arm, wishing I could find Abd al-Malik: he would welcome me with open arms; he would manage to find me some work.

I hold onto a final vestige of hope, but it dies as the amulet fails to procure any work for me. In a loud voice, I curse the market and all its traders and spices. I curse the injustice and the demons of this world. I left my family under hunger's dominion, and came here to provide them with money for food. I was forced to steal, yet when I gave up theft to look for proper work I found that all paths to an honest living were blocked.

I will be forced to steal again, and this time I will not regret it: Theft is no crime for those who truly know hunger.

That night I make my way from the cinema to the fuul restaurant, and from there to the spice market, intending to steal some spices and sell them the next day. The shopkeepers do not fully close up their stores at night, and I think I can sneak in and out without any trouble, for no one sleeps in the souk and the whole place is empty at night. I have grown accustomed to stealing in the past two months, and this should not be too difficult for me.

I sneak into the souk carrying some paper bags. Night's dark robes provide ample cover—I cannot even see my hands in front of my face. Yet my many daytime visits here have taught me where each alley leads, where each shop is to be found.

I easily manage to open up the first shop. I grope among the sacks of spices in the darkness and tensely fill my bags in haste. One sack contains dried hibiscus, another fenugreek, another corn. I feel my way through them, placing my full bags by the door of the shop. I become greedy though, and as I look to fill up my very last bag, I unfortunately open a sack of chili powder. The powder fills my nostrils as I unwittingly scoop out a handful of the stuff, and I start to cough and sneeze as never before. I manage to muffle some of my sneezing, but not all of it. I quickly pick up my bags and close the shop behind me, hurrying on my way, coughing and spitting as I run.

The souk is large, with many long alleyways. I hear the sound of footsteps coming toward me from the top of one of the alleys, so I hide by one of the stores and desperately try to stem the sneezing and coughing, but a few suppressed coughs still sneak out of me. I stare vainly into the darkness, then try to see with my ears.

Suddenly I hear someone sneezing from within the shop beside me. The sneezing worsens, and I am afraid that it might be coming from one of the shopkeepers. I set off again, running recklessly through the market like a terrified rabbit, no longer caring about whether I crash into someone, for fear can sometimes be a source of boldness.

The crisis is over at the end of the alley. My breathing is raspy from the chili, the fear, and the running, but I have finally reached the far end of the souk, and am now on the edge of one of the public parks where I had slept the past few days. I broke one of the lamps there so I could sleep in peace, away from the prying eyes of the police and the biting mosquitoes.

I take up my spot in the garden, setting the bag of chili a few meters away from me beside the stone wall crowned with iron bars that surrounds the park. Using the bag of hibiscus as a pillow, I lay down and think about what I have done. I laugh out loud when I recall the sudden sneezing of the stranger: Maybe it was someone just like me, someone else seeking his share in the dark, I say to myself. My sleep is troubled that night. A policeman keeps coming to me in my dreams, arresting me over and over again.

I wake the next morning and try to stir up some energy, but my body is weak and my bones feel as flimsy as paper. I take my stolen spices to the fruit and vegetable market, sit down there and begin to sell.

At first, my presence startles both the shopkeepers and the customers, but the women slowly begin to buy my spices, for mine are cheaper than those at the spice market.

I do not lower the prices too much, though, to avoid casting suspicion on myself. Sometimes I hold my ground when the customers haggle over the cost of something, but other times I drop the price a bit, and pretend to be losing money on the sale. And so I learn the art of illegal commerce. At night I go about stealthily acquiring my merchandise, coughing and sneezing my way through the empty spice market. And in the morning I return to the fruit and vegetable market to sell my goods, very much in line with my colleague al-Khattaf's theory of equitable distribution.

After much time and practice, I no longer cough or sneeze, nor do I run through the alleys of the souk, but rather proceed calmly about my business. I begin to make some money, and I also move from my spot in the park to the ruins of a shack behind the camel market that is only ever approached by stray dogs, or by some drunkard coming by to vomit or piss on one of the ramshackle walls. The smell is horrible here, but I have trained my nose well, and now it only smells what I want it to.

I send my mother a fair amount of money this time, and once again ask if there are any letters for me at the post office. A letter from my mother has finally arrived, written by Sheikh al-Faki: The first transfer of money was received, and my mother is well, as are my two sisters. My mother also wishes me success in the city, and asks about what I am doing, and how I am, and where exactly I am staying.

This is my first true moment of happiness in the city. I can smell the scent of Wad al-Nar on the paper, the scent of my mother. And as I walk by the kebab restaurant, smoke gets in my eyes, and I wipe away two warm tears. I walk the whole way back singing old songs that I had made up in my days in the village. So many cherished memories come back to me. The palm tree. The wars of stones with the other children. Sitting in front of the house. Playing with Halima. My graveyard sanctuary. Abd al-Malik's family. Sheikh al-Faki. My mother and Karima, then Halima once again.

The other traders at the market gradually grow accustomed to my presence. Had I been selling fruits and vegetables like the rest, some of them might have had a problem with my being there. But it is possible that my selling spices has attracted some more customers to the area and thus actually helped some of the traders' sales. In any case, they have become more comfortable with my being there, and I too begin to feel at ease among them. Sometimes they even ask for my help in unloading produce from the delivery trucks, for which I always receive some fruits and vegetables as compensation. I think of my mother and my sisters each time this happens, though—I cannot help but feel guilty whenever I eat something that they cannot.

One day the man known as al-Kayyal—'the weigher'—pays me a visit. He is one of the more important shopkeepers in the souk. He is a bit past forty years old, tall, and has a thin mustache and a jagged face like that of a falcon. He is irritable and quick to anger, and also quick of step. During my first few days at the souk he used to look at me every morning as if I were an insect. I tried to win him over with smiles and friendly greetings, but that only made him even more severe and surly. He approaches me as I sit amid my spices, and begins the interrogation, "What's your name?"

"Hamza."

"Where do you live?"

"I don't have a place to live yet—I'm new to the city."

"Where are you from?"

"I'm from a village called Wad al-Nar hundreds of miles from here."

"And why have you come here?"

"To try my luck and see if I can't find some work to help support my family. Things have gotten much worse in our village since the famine set in, and there's no work there."

"And how much do you make from this work of yours?"

"Enough to survive. I live out in the open, and whatever money I have left over I send to my mother."

"Is your father alive?"

"I don't know. He abandoned us years ago and we don't know where he is."

He interrupts me with a cough and stares at me from where he is standing. I too am standing, but his harsh gaze makes me feel as if I am sitting on the ground. He continues his interrogation, "Don't you want better work?"

"What work? Of course I do. Do you have something for me?"

"You said that you're all alone here, and that you don't have a place to stay. Well, you can work in my store, and also live in it. I'll pay you each month according to how well you work."

"Alright. When can I start working?"

"Right away. Gather up these bags of yours and follow me to the store. But you should know that I'll be testing you out at first, and watching how well you work."

Al-Kayyal sets off ahead of me, leaving me to my joy, one known only to those who have truly tasted danger, hunger, and fear. Finding some honest work and a safe place to stay has put me in high spirits, and I am determined to give the new job my all. I work hard, hoping to gain al-Kayyal's acceptance and thus keep the job. My curiosity grows with each passing day—I want to know how much he is going to pay me. The whole month I work like an ant before the onset of winter, as if the store were my own, as if I were al-Kayyal's partner. I unload the fruits and vegetables from the delivery trucks, arrange them in the store, and spray them with water. I call out to each passerby, shouting and singing the praises of my produce. This is not the usual way of doing things in the souk. More women begin to come to the store. They enjoy talking to me and always laugh at my strange accent, and also at the way I sometimes slip up when trying to imitate the speech of the city. I befriend many of the customers—young and old, men and women—and start to truly enjoy my work. I finally see approval in al-Kayyal's eyes and my hopes soar, but they are dashed when he pays me half of what I used to make from selling spices.

I am not too upset about my pay, though. I give up some of my pastimes, for example my frequent trips to the cinema, which I now only go to once a week. And I start eating only fruits and vegetables, always cooking them myself. I thus manage to spend only about a third of my pay on myself, and every month I go to the post office and send my mother the rest of the money. Despite my having worked as a thief, and in spite of al-Kayyal's clear stinginess and his constant complaints about how poor the business is doing, I do not want to rob the man who has provided me shelter me by letting me stay at his store.

I get used to beginning work early in the morning and finishing it shortly before sunset, according to al-Kayyal's wishes. Our store is the only one in the whole souk that stays open so late, for the customers mostly only come in the morning or around midday—far fewer people show up after that, and between early afternoon and sunset there is hardly enough business to justify the store's staying open.

I learn a lot about al-Kayyal, not from him but from his second wife. She comes to the store every day and works with me, sometimes for as long as three or four hours, and always in the presence of al-Kayyal. In the beginning I can sense him watching me, following my eyes, my movements, and my speech. But once he has assured himself of my harmlessness, once he realizes that I am just a naïve villager who knows nothing about women, he permits his wife to come to the store in his absence.

She is twenty-six years old and quite slender. Two large eyes and a small mouth with a tattoo beneath it adorn her face. She has smooth skin, a sweet voice, and an exquisite smell. Her name is Hayah. "I married him over seven years ago," she tells me, "after his first wife had come down with a severe case of malaria, which wrecked her pale body and turned her into an old maid while she was still young. Her second offense was not to have borne him any children."

Hayah stops talking, and remains silent for quite a while. I consider changing the subject, thinking that she does not want to unload all her sorrows and sufferings on me. But then she lets out a deep sigh, stares blankly in front of her, and continues in an angry tone, "I didn't know he was already married. My father wanted to marry me off to the very first man to come knocking on our door, in order to lessen his own burdens. He had seven daughters, of whom two were already married at the time—I became the third. After me, he married off three of my sisters in two years, but he has yet to get rid of his last daughter. Most of our marriages are not particularly happy, mainly because of my father's haste. We were always just burdens for him—that's his way of seeing things. It's as if we'd jumped out of our mother's womb of our own free will, with him having had no hand in the matter."

She continues talking while her hand plays around in the piles of fruits and vegetables; she reorganizes them, improving their appearance, while I nod my head and listen to her, putting back whatever produce falls to the ground. She continues, "He was kind during his first year with me, but then his tenderness and affection turned into dislike and cruelty, and things grew worse between us. He accused me of being barren. I was patient and put up with it for a long time, but when his hatred became too much for me to take, I tried to go back to my father. He wanted nothing to do with me, though, and brought me straight back to my husband. I lived with al-Kayyal under one roof. I endured his hatred in the morning and suffered his cruelty in the evening. He dragged me to his bed whenever he wanted me, uttering a few insincere words of affection. This would all end a couple minutes later, when he'd give me his back and go to sleep. My blood would boil at the sound of his snoring."

While talking, she begins mixing the fruits and vegetables together without realizing it. She continues, "The situation worsened after he got married for the third time in two years, this time to a woman who was twenty-two years old. He treated her like a saint, and threw me out of his house and into the one where his first wife was living. You might think that the relationship between me and his first wife would be a bit strained, but that wasn't at all the case. We became friends, for both of us had experienced the same pain; we'd both drunk from the same cup. The only difference between me and his new wife is that I didn't know that he was already married, though I believe my father did. And although al-Kayyal makes quite a lot of money, he's very tightfisted, always pretending to be in financial difficulty—you've seen this yourself. His first wife and I live on his handouts. I can't return to my family, but I send them whatever money I have left over. I never finished my education, because my father would not pay for it, claiming that supporting seven daughters was hard enough already. My husband is my fate now. He's my guardian in the eyes of both religion and the law, and trying to divorce him would be useless."

Hayah stops talking and looks at what she has done with the fruits and vegetables. She laughs bitterly while tears stream down her cheeks. She shakes her head, unable to believe what has happened—and is happening—to her. I hold my tongue and refrain from asking any questions. I too begin to play around with the produce. It hurts me to hear Hayah's words, and the more her story brings us together, the more I despise al-Kayyal.

Hayah and I grow ever closer. We tell each other everything. And as time passes I begin to develop real feelings for her. She opened up her heart and listened to my story, a story that no one else had ever shown any interest in. She begins to come to the store every day; these visits ease the pain I feel from being so far from home, and soothe some of my suffering.

Business begins to flourish—my strange, distinctive accent attracts both men and women to the store. The customers are also very fond of Hayah—she is charming to the older customers and playful with the younger ones. And as the sales increase, so do the profits. My pay, however, remains the same, but I do not grumble or complain, for Hayah has given me a new life. And whenever she is late coming to the store, I grow anxious, and a nervous tone informs my voice as I call out to the customers.

We become increasingly warm and affectionate with each other. She finds peace in my presence, and I find peace in hers. She spends long hours at the store, often staying past sunset—I much prefer this to any trips to the cinema or strolls through the city.

The advent of winter means I spend most evenings in the store. Visions of Hayah fill my dreams. She seems to be showing me more than merely friendly interest. I can sense her gazing at me, flustering me with her eyes. I love her. I feel love for the very first time. My heart trembles, my pulse races, my voice shakes. I experience the despairing, expectant sighs of love. I come to know its tender glances. I feel young. I feel strong and weak at one and the same time. But in spite of my natural boldness, I do not reveal my thoughts to her—she is married and under the charge of another man, a fact that only serves to increase my misery and hopelessness.

That idiot is burying this sweet rose, trampling her beauty. His ignorance is forcing all of us into uncharted waters. I am consumed by jealousy, by my agonizing desire for Hayah, and my unfulfilled love for her. I go mad every Thursday, the one day of the week when al-Kayyal visits her and stays with her until the next morning. I cannot understand why he does this, for he never shows her any true affection. Is it simply habit? Is he trying to exercise his rights as a husband, trying to prove his power and manhood? Is it a sign of psychological weakness, a certain dementia? Whatever the case, Hayah has entered my heart, and now my mind can find no peace.

A cold night. I sit and listen to the radio, to songs by Muhammad al-Amin that match my pain and sorrow, my secret love. I hear someone knocking on the tin door of the store, so I light the kerosene lamp. "Who's there?" I ask. A familiar voice answers, a voice I had—before today—so often longed to hear. Hayah enters quickly, unfolding the part of her long robe that covers her head. "I was visiting some friends who live near the market," she says, "and I thought I'd come by and see how you're doing."

She loves me. I had both hoped and feared that this would happen. It is not my love for her that frightens me, but rather the act of expressing it. I try to swallow my feelings whenever they rise to my throat. I fear my tongue may lose its grip and reveal my heart to her. But when she declares her feelings to me, the only thing left for me to do is let out everything in my heart in one burst, like a sneeze brought on by a single speck of dust.

She is sitting by where I usually sleep, without speaking. I feel uneasy, so I ask her if she wants anything. She takes my hand, and I sit down beside her. The lamp behind me casts a weak light on her face. It is as if I am seeing her for the very first time, as if all of this is a beautiful dream. Yet I do not want to spoil or corrupt her, so I let go of her hand.

I wake up before dawn. The smell of perfume and sandalwood fills the store where we are still covered in warmth. The sounds of dawn outside announce the birth of new day, and also something that I have never known before: a deep love; a coming together; both courage and fear, joy and remorse. My mind and heart begin to spin. And Hayah comes to me every night, except on Thursdays.

Amidst the fruits and vegetables, her suffering finds company in my own. Our love, so forbidden yet so true, lives among the crates in the dim light of a kerosene lamp. We whisper guiltily in the darkness. The vision of my mother visits me in my sleep, asking me how I am doing and telling me to come home. But Hayah's whisperings soothe my troubled ears with the sweetest of words, while my heart quivers like a fish out of water. The days and weeks go by.

Two months after that first night, Hayah comes to the store earlier than normal, unusually sullen and quiet. After a long silence, she says, "Hamza, I'm pregnant."

A new tone informs my voice as I sing to the customers, and my playful lightheartedness turns into anxiety. But al-Kayyal is overjoyed to learn that Hayah is pregnant. He brings her to live with him again, swapping her with his newer wife, who had lost some of her glamour after the first year and had become the latest to be accused of barrenness. In his joy, al-Kayyal increases my pay and starts to treat me better. The man is finally going to become a father, after having suffered through all the swindling doctors and women. He says the same thing every time he sees me now, "You're a bringer of good fortune. It was your coming here that blessed us, and I won't ever do without you." His sullenness has turned into joy and cheer, while my joy has become resentment and hate.

The most merciless blow of all, however, comes from Hayah: She stops visiting me, no longer comes by to ask how I am doing. Al-Kayyal's happiness and sudden affection for have overwhelmed her and made her forget about the real father of her child. I hear from the other women that she is queen of the household again, that al-Kayyal is at her every beck and call, and will not even let her drink a cup of water on her own. All of this has caused her to forget Hamza and his love, his longing and his fruit. She knows that in a whole lifetime he still would not be able to provide her with what al-Kayyal can give her in a single week. So she casts Hamza from her mind, and never shows up at the souk anymore.

I am in agony, but going to see her or announcing the truth of the matter would cause a scandal that would ruin all of us. I long for my village. I have arrived at a crossroads, caught between the wreckage of the past and an aimless future, while the present slowly, mercilessly gnaws on my living flesh.

I contrive a big argument with al-Kayyal in order to leave the store. I send half of the money I had saved to my mother in the village, then go to the passport office and obtain a permit to travel to Egypt. At first I believe it to be a passport, but I later learn that it is actually a new permit called the Nile Valley Card that only allows its holder to move between Sudan and Egypt. After this, I buy a ticket for the train heading to Wadi Halfa.

For the second time in my life I get on a train—this time with two burdens in my mind—and think about the unknown life that lies before me. After long hours lost in thought amid the dust and din, I arrive at my destination. I do not stay at a hotel, but prefer to lie down with my shadow in the moonlight, waiting in the open air for the steamer that will come tomorrow and travel to the High Dam.

I lie down alone on the sand. I can hear women laughing and men coughing, babies crying, youths joking about—yet I remain in an agonizing state of silence. The next day I spit more than I speak, and spend more time waving my hands in disgust than I do greeting people. I curse this life, I curse everything in it. I left Wad al-Nar to escape its fire, only to find the whole world ablaze. I left my village bearing the burden of my mother and two sisters, and today I am leaving the country with a new one—that of a child who has yet to be born. I am leaving before I hear its voice in the world, for its mother has cast me aside and there is nothing I can do.

The steamer arrives the next day. After the usual formalities I go on board, carrying my old bag made of palm fronds and some clothes, along with my amulet that I still wear to protect me from danger and the unknown.

The ship's horn announces its departure. I lie down on the deck and finally fall into an exhausted sleep. I wake to the sound of a child crying and the smell of bread. For a moment I think that my mother is baking again, and that it is Halima who is crying, but when I stand up I see a group of young men eating. They invite me to share in the meal, so I sit down and begin devouring the bread, which I dip into a spicy okra sauce. I drink a cup of tea after the meal, lost in my sad thoughts. The others notice this and try to cheer me up, and they keep trying until they succeed in dragging me out of my desolation and into their circle. In an effort to forget myself, I sing some songs by al-Amin and Abd al-Aziz al-Mubarak, songs that I had committed to memory in the days when I used to listen to Abd al-Malik's family radio.

I find the group larger the next evening, and they start clapping to get me to sing again. I sing out of pain, and in it as well. I do not forget my troubles, but perhaps it is this that makes my voice deeper, more stirring. The group of young men nickname me "al-Fannan"—'the artist'—then they ask me about where I plan to go. I tell them that I have no specific destination, for this is my first trip to Egypt.

At night I climb to the deck of the steamer to sit alone and look at the broad Nile in the moonlight. The deck of the ship is warm, and when I lay down on it I see nothing but the glow of the stars in the night sky. I think of how far I have come since I left my village, now so long ago. I want to wake up from this never-ending nightmare; I bang my head a few times on the deck of the steamer but to no avail.

I look at the stars once again, and recognize some of the constellations. They are the same stars I used to see in Wad al-Nar. Yes, I have often seen this incomplete square of light from my village, and also that luminous ring over there. It is a great comfort to find something constant and unchanging in this world. Yet I can feel the scattered strangeness of the earth running beneath my feet, carrying me to some new place where an unknown fate awaits me.

To Another City

And so I arrive in Egypt and set foot in this land of legend, this country Sheikh al-Faki had told me so much about. Who in our village would believe that I am here? Sheikh al-Faki himself would not believe it, and if he did find out he would probably go into shock, for he was the only explorer ever to venture out of the village, and he would not be pleased with insignificant Hamza undertaking a voyage reserved for more prominent people.

These thoughts pass through my mind as I leave the border control area and head to the broad open area behind the port to look for a bathroom. I see the scattered silhouettes of people at the far end of the place. Some of them are standing up like lofty palms, and others are squatting. At first I think that they are praying, but then why wouldn't everyone be praying together? When I get closer I realize what they are doing and, picking a spot a little way from the others, follow their lead.

Feeling hungry, I head to a coffeehouse where men are sitting in small close-knit groups, most of them discussing business and arguing about money and wages. An elderly man is sitting at the front, his rickety chair held together with twine. There is an old desk with a single drawer in front of him, and a tray holding a cup of tea on top of the desk. One woman and a couple of men are standing there. He is changing money for them, taking their Sudanese dinars and giving them Egyptian pounds. I sit down to order something to eat, but they have nothing but cookies here. I order a few of them, which fail to sate my hunger. The high prices keep me from ordering any more, however.

I stay there a while and watch the people as they talk in many different dialects, most of which I cannot understand. Then I fall asleep for a bit, my head resting on the small table in front of me. The waiter wakes me though, and puts another cup of tea in front of me. When I tell him that I did not order one, he replies, "You can't sit here for free."

It is eleven o'clock in the morning, but the train will not be coming until two in the afternoon. I sit up in my chair and sip my tea extremely slowly. The waiter watches the liquid sink in the cup, and as soon as it is empty he pounces on me with another one. I know I will have to pay for it, but I do not object. I sip the tea like a suckling child, trying to ignore the waiter. He hovers around me like a kite bird, singing some songs that I cannot fully understand, but that somehow seem to be mocking me, putting me ill at ease.

I leave the café a half-hour later, paying the bill on the way out. Now the waiter can finally have some peace from me, and I from him.

One of the young men from the steamer calls out to me from a distance. I see the group sitting in a circle and drinking tea. They invite me to have some tea and pass the time with them until the train comes. They seem different now, more serious, though I am not sure if this is due to the tiring journey or to concerns about work. They are quite a vagabondish group—I had noticed this while we were still on the ship. After a while, I leave to explore the area a bit before the train comes, telling them that I will be back soon.

I walk around the place and look at everything like an innocent child seeing the world for the very first time. My eyes are curious, as are my ears and nose—all my senses are filled with curiosity. I think of my mother and sisters, and wonder how they are doing and how things are in the village. I continue walking, keeping track of the way for fear of getting lost, even though the place really is not that big. I look at the watch—Abd al-Malik's watch—to check the time. I regret not having found him in the city, and sadly remember how his entire family left the village, leaving nothing behind but memories; memories and an old watch very dear to me.

Time passes slowly. It keeps getting hotter, until there is nothing else to do but go back to the coffeehouse and order a bottle of cola from the waiter. It occurs to me that he looks a bit like a frog, though I am not sure what has left me with this impression—his obnoxious behavior, perhaps. He sees me and quickly makes some room for me to sit. I order my drink. He asks if I am hungry but I say no, so he quickly brings me the cola. Then the frog proceeds to stare fixedly at the bottle until the time comes to leap at me with another one, both of us enjoying this new game—'drink and jump'—together. Indeed, it seems to be the waiter's favorite pastime. Perhaps it is his physique that reminds me of a frog, or the way he springs from one table to another, bringing the customers more tea, cola, and coffee even though they have not ordered any of it. It could also be his scheming eyes that pop out of their sockets just a little more than they should, or his hoarse and croaking voice. Or maybe it is all of this together.

I pass the time with this silent game, and drink three bottles of cola while laughing bitterly to myself. I leave around one in the afternoon. The frog croaks mockingly in my face as I go.

I return to the group, and sit and talk with them a bit. They begin to gather up their things, and I help them carry their stuff to the train station, for I have very little with me: the bag made of palm fronds, a new travel permit, a little money, an old watch, and an amulet that never leaves my neck.

The train arrives and we quickly get on. Yet it remains at the station for a long time, and does not get going until half past three. My curiosity starts up with the train, and I peer out the window to observe this new world.

It takes more than fifteen hours for us to travel from the High Dam to Cairo—my neck and back ache the whole way because of the train's crooked wooden seats. Although I am tired, I keep my eyes open the whole time to take in the sights, even after nightfall. I notice the same phenomenon that I had observed on my first voyage: the farther north I go, the more signs of life there are.

I arrive in Cairo at four o'clock in the morning. Three of the young men suggest that we all go sleep in one of the cheap hotels that they know of, and I agree. We walk down a long side street filled with shops and coffeehouses—some of which are still open at that late hour of the night—until we arrive at the hotel.

This is the first time in my entire life that I have ever had a bed. I want to sleep on the ground, since that is what I am used to and what feels most natural. Moreover, I tend to move around a lot in my sleep, and I am afraid of falling off this strange box. But my exhaustion makes the decision for me: I fall asleep on the bed.

I wake up the next afternoon to the din of the city. I am alone in the room, but I find a note from my three friends. They decided to let me rest from the long journey. One of them will be back in the afternoon to show me around Cairo a bit, and after that we will all have dinner together. I want to see the street and the crowds in the daylight, but because our room is on the back side of the hotel, all I can see from the window is a narrow alley flanked by tall houses. I go to the bathroom to take a cold bath, and feel the water drip from my head and body as I get out. I put my clothes on my wet body after I clean some of the dust off of them. They do not smell very good, but they are all I have.

When Abd al-Malik's watch points to one o'clock, al-Khidr—a young man from the group I was with—enters the room and greets me, "Let's go get something to eat."

We go down to the street and I see it for the first time during the day. It reminds me of a beehive, so full of movement and activity. I look at all the people as I walk, craning my neck forward and backward while al-Khidr desperately tries to drag and shove me along. He laughs and says, "There's a lot to see here. But let's go eat now—aren't you hungry yet?" I give no answer. I am in the state that I was in when I visited Khartoum and Omdurman for the first time. I walk slowly, turning my head at every motion or noise. I observe the faces of the men, women, and children. I examine their clothes and listen to them talk, and all the while al-Khidr drags me on like a beast to the slaughter.

We walk to a restaurant only about a hundred meters away from the hotel, but I feel as if I see all of Egypt in this short distance. Finally, we sit down to eat. In my curiosity and delight, I had forgotten how hungry I was. I devour a few fuul and falafel sandwiches—which would later become an addiction for me—then drink a cup of sugarcane juice. Al-Khidr insists on paying for my meal that day.

We walk to the end of the road, which marks the beginning of a large outdoor market filled with people selling fabric, clothes, and many other things. We cross through it until we come to an area called Khan al-Khalili. There we find the rest of the group sitting in a coffeehouse on a sloping, cloth-covered alleyway too narrow for two people to walk side by side. We sit and have a drink with them. A good-humored man in a clean white robe approaches our table, laughing. They begin bargaining, and keep at it until everyone is in agreement. Then my friends pull out some gold and silver that they had smuggled across the border, and they conclude the transaction. I now understand why they had been so nervous before getting off the ship to go through customs, as well as the tense conversation they had afterward. We leave the coffeehouse together with all of them happy, though I myself am a bit taken aback.

"We are inviting you out to eat," one of them tells me. "The food at this place is so good that you will be dreaming about it for the rest of your life."

We enter the restaurant. It is one of those places where the food's aroma seems to pull at all the passersby, the kind of place that so often torments those with a strong sense of smell, such as myself. Kebab and kofta are being grilled on charcoals—it is the most delicious meal I have ever had. I had seen places like this in Khartoum and Omdurman, but the high prices always kept me away.

My mind wanders a lot during the meal. I think about the old days in the village, when I was young and times were better. This very same food could be smelled at the festivals and weddings. I used to eat food like this. What happened to the bounty of our village? Drought has erased these sweet memories from my mind; famine has taken hold of our village. We are happy just to have some plain bread these days. I wonder what my mother and sisters are eating right now. Have they received the money I sent them? I cannot shake off these questions, and as the time and distance between me and my family grows, so does my fear for them.

The worst thing for me is not having a permanent address, not being able to receive any letters to comfort me, to ease my mind. I think about the long months that I have been away from home. I think about Omdurman, that city of love and painful memories. In a few months, I will become a father, a father to a child I will not see. And here I am trying to support my family even though I am barely able to support myself. I can feel these thoughts suffocating me, choking my hopes. All the old questions return: Have I done the right thing? Was it truly necessary for me to make this journey? Was it the correct decision, or have I made a big mistake?

Suddenly I hear someone's voice persistently trying to get my attention, "Hamza. Hamza! What's wrong? Why aren't you eating?"

"What?"

"You're eating so slowly, and not saying a word. You seem sad."

"It's nothing. I'm fine. I'm just a bit overwhelmed by this place."

"You'll get used to everything here. If you were worrying about work, then you can stop right now. We've decided that you should stay with us—we could use you."

I answer doubtfully, "What kind of work are you offering me?"

The conversation becomes serious, the others join in, and the laughter gradually dies down. The three start telling me about their work. I set aside my other thoughts for a while and focus on the conversation. To an unemployed man like me, an offer of work is music to the ears. The type of work is not important. Finding work—any work—is all that matters.

The four of us travel to Port Said in a luxurious passenger bus and have no trouble entering the duty-free city. I see a large souk that seems to span almost the entire city. I see stores, trucks, vendors, men, women, children, electrical appliances, and clothes. In the stores and out on the street everyone is trying on clothes, and all the vendors call out, trying to sell their goods. I often stop to see the action, and a vendor courteously tugs at my hand, urging me to buy some trousers and a shirt from him. He traps me in a corner, "Just try them on!" he says. "It doesn't cost anything to try them on!" I become so flustered that one of my colleagues has to pull me away, thanking the vendor for me. But a couple moments later I fall into the hands of a man selling electrical appliances, and suddenly I find myself holding a radio. "I don't want one!" I yell, and the price is cut in half. "I don't need one!" The price is halved again. I laugh when the man tells me what a bargain I am getting.

Al-Khidr pulls me away, saying, "If you're not careful, you'll wind up buying everything in the souk!" I laugh at all of this—it seems so strange and interesting. This is a living souk, a place of madness and wonder. I hear people singing and joking around with each other. I hear arguments, people haggling over prices, agreeing on prices—the sound of sales being made. I have never seen so much hustle and bustle before, not even in my first two days in Cairo.

My companions have a few specific stores that they always go to. In each of them they bargain over everything, and the shopkeepers never get upset or angry about this. Rather, they seem to enjoy the bargaining, which is always a very prolonged affair. At some point my colleagues usually leave the store, whereupon the shopkeeper draws them back in with kind words, and the bargaining resumes.

I laugh as I look at this wondrous new place, and think back to the souk in Omdurman. In our country, if anyone even tries to bargain over something, the shopkeeper turns his back on him, or starts stacking stuff, or simply sits down on a chair without replying. The shopkeepers in our country never tolerate any bargaining, and if you test their will on the matter they will refuse to sell you anything at all for the rest of the day, even if you come back and offer to pay twice the usual price.

This is such a strange world. I used to think that Egypt was exactly the same as Sudan, but so many things are different here. I am beginning to learn how to deal with this new society, how to fit in a little bit. I do not want anyone here to think of me as a foreigner, even if I am one.

The bargaining ends, though I do not know in whose favor. Everyone seems happy, and my colleagues begin changing clothes, putting on their new ones: jeans and brightly colored shirts, just like the stuff the cowboys wore in the movies I used to watch in Omdurman. My colleagues want me to put some of them on, and I laugh out loud as I do so: I cannot help but think about how I must look in these new clothes. I used to imagine myself as a cowboy after coming out of the movie theater; I used to picture myself in cowboy clothes on a horse with a shotgun or pistol. Now the only things missing are the gun and the horse.

My laughter spreads and infects the others—though they do not know why they are laughing—until even the shopkeeper joins in.

After I finish putting on these new clothes, which feel very tight on me, the others ask me to carry a large bag filled with many more clothes of all different sizes. We spend the rest of the day in the city, each of us with a bag in hand. We go to a fish restaurant and then to a coffeehouse, and I keep stopping along the way to talk and laugh with the shopkeepers. I forget my homesickness a little, and begin to feel a bit closer to this new world.

I notice something strange on our way back: Everyone in this city is wearing bright new clothes. Some people are even walking around with the price tag still hanging from their collars, or the label still stuck to the back pockets of their trousers. I see some toys and games for sale and stop to look at them, wanting to buy something for Halima and Karima. But as usual, my colleagues drag me on before I can buy anything, while I keep thinking about a doll that I had seen, and about Halima.

I feel a certain joy when I look at this city, especially after al-Khidr tells me of its brave past and its resistance throughout the war. He tells me how much the city has changed in recent years, explaining that it was turned into a duty-free zone, and that ever since then its port has been attracting trade from both Europe and Asia. He keeps talking about the city, and in the middle of all these stories I ask myself: Will my village ever be able to start anew like this? We're in the middle of a war, the worst kind of war a city or village can be subjected to. Will a smile will ever return to the faces there?

I touch my amulet, wishing for my village to recover from its disease, hoping to one day see it like this wondrous city.

The others tell me it is time for us to return. We quickly leave the city behind and start down a long path that leads to the customs area. Before we reach customs, however, we turn off the path to a large side area where many people of all ages have stopped. All of them are taking off their old clothes and putting on new ones; the others explain that they are preparing to go through customs.

We are running late, and the last bus to Cairo will be leaving soon. The other three ask me to put on the clothes remaining in my bag, one on top of the other, so that we will not have to pay any fees. They quickly put on their own clothes and go on ahead, while I stay behind and clumsily dress myself, not knowing that some of the clothes are on backward and some inside out, so that I look like a clown from one of the movies I used to watch.

I run after them, and am the last of the group to arrive in the customs line. The others all pass through quickly, but some rough people push their way in front of me before I can reach the front of the line. I let them go ahead, and then even more people start cutting in front of me until I find myself standing at the very back of the line again. After that I stop letting people in front of me. Then another man tries to push his way in front of me and we get into an argument. A customs officer hears us, pulls us both out the line, and puts us at the very back. This only makes me angrier, and I start cursing. No one understands my dialect though, and some of the others in line laugh at me. I curse the lot of them in my rage, but this only makes them laugh even more. Finally I shut up, at a loss as to what to do.

Al-Khidr appears on the other side of the customs area and signals for me to hurry, for the bus will be leaving soon. At that moment I see that one of the young customs inspectors has begun moving through the line to check people. He orders some of them to take off their clothes, swearing at them and counting the articles, and then forces them to pay the required fee. While this is happening I manage to slip quickly to the front of the line, and finally make it out. I sigh in relief as the others say to me, "Getting out of here's not quite as simple as getting in." Suddenly they stop in their tracks, and all three of them look at me in amazement, laughing and pointing at me. "What is it?" I yell. "What are you laughing at?" They are laughing so hard now that they are falling on the ground. Then they get up and, still laughing, run for the bus while I angrily run after them.

I sit at the back amid the many bags, and the smell of new clothes fills the entire bus. "You're a lucky man," my companions say to me. "We were in such a hurry that we forgot to tell you how to put on the clothes."

I am wearing everything the wrong way. I have all the clothes on inside-out, with the more transparent ones on top of the others, so that everyone could easily see how many pieces of clothing I had on my body—no detailed inspection was necessary. I look like a multicolored carpet. And as for the four pairs of pants, I laugh about them even more than the others do.

We continue laughing and telling jokes, playing around and singing all the way to Cairo. Then we go back to the hotel to sleep, picking up some fuul and falafel sandwiches on the way, which we eat in the room while recalling the day's events.

The next day, we head to the big souk in the middle of the city. We stand on the street and sell our new products, and I gain my first hands-on experience in the art of protracted bargaining. I learn the ropes on my very first day on the job, and my old smile returns to me.

The bond between me and my three colleagues grows ever deeper. We travel to Port Said every three days, then sell the products in the market in Cairo. I find myself enjoying the work, especially the bargaining.

The time comes for us to travel back to Sudan, for we had agreed that I would help them smuggle gold and silver as well. The procedure is an interesting one. First we travel to the High Dam, and from there to Wadi Halfa; then on to Khartoum, and finally to the souk in Omdurman where the silver and gold are to be bought. On each trip two people wait at the High Dam while the other two travel on to Omdurman and then return with the gold and silver—they know how to smuggle it across the border without getting caught. We alternate roles with each trip until my turn comes to go to the souk at Omdurman.

While there, I visit the fruit and vegetable market to see how things are, and find that al-Kayyal has closed his store and gone to the town of Karima to open up a new shop. Short on time, I somewhat brashly ask about his wife. The reply I receive is both easier and harder than I had expected: al-Kayyal divorced Hayah after she had a miscarriage, citing irreconcilable differences. I can feel the world spinning around me, its images all shaken now. I walk through the streets in a daze, thinking about my time in Omdurman, and about Hayah. Something of our first love still beats in my heart, in spite of the bitterness and all the time that has passed. I long more than ever to return to my village, but there is not enough time. Traveling there would take at least two days, and al-Khidr is here with me, and the other two are waiting for us at the High Dam.

I send some money to my mother. I had thought that coming back here would bring me joy, but it has only caused me more suffering. I return with al-Khidr to the High Dam, and from there we all go back to Cairo.

My companions decide to undertake a larger operation, in which all of us would travel together to Sudan. I tell them that I do not want to go this time, and they are split over my refusal. One of them thinks that I am afraid, another that I enjoy being poor. Al-Khidr is on my side, however. "What harm is done if he doesn't take part?" he asks the other two. "He can stay here and wait for us, and continue smuggling goods between Port Said and Cairo."

The three set out, and I wait eighteen days for them at the hotel, during which time I make three trips to Port Said, always returning to sell the goods in Cairo. On the last of these trips I buy the doll that I had seen for Halima, and another one for Karima. I have enough money to stay at the hotel for just one month. During the day I walk through the streets of Cairo, taking in all the noise and frantic activity, and marveling at the way of life here. I walk to the most distant parts of the city, wanting to discover everything. And every evening I return to the hotel, dragging my feet in exhaustion.

My colleagues had told me they would return in ten days, but now eighteen days have gone by and there is still no sign of them. I begin to worry, fearing the worst. I want to go to the High Dam to find out what has happened to them, but I do not have enough money for such a long trip. Instead, I decide to wait at the hotel another three days, during which I do not venture outside very much. I do occasionally go out to drink tea or buy some fuul and falafel sandwiches, and I still go for walks in the evening—yet even then I never stray from the street the hotel is on, but walk up and down it like a chained animal.

Three weeks have gone by without any word, and I begin to lose hope. Something must have happened to them. What can I do by myself here, a stranger in this new city? I have enough money to stay at the hotel for another week, but after that I will be thrown out onto the street.

The month of waiting comes to an end, and with it my last remaining hopes of ever seeing my colleagues again. I wander aimlessly through the Cairo streets asking for work. I come across a Sudanese man in one of the large souks. He is selling Sudanese goods, and I ask him if he knows how I can find some work. He gives me an address in a district of Cairo called Ain Shams where there is a large Sudanese community. I find several Sudanese social clubs there and ask if they have any jobs for me. The best I can do is work in exchange for lodging at one of the clubs. I stay there a few weeks, cleaning the club and bringing tea and coffee to the guests, and barely earn enough money to buy my fuul and falafel sandwiches.

I am worried that nothing will change here, and that things will get even worse for my mother while I am stuck here, dazed and confused. Some suggest that I should try to get a passport from the embassy, which might allow me to travel to some of the other Arab countries. Hope returns once more, and I go to the embassy to ask about getting a passport. They tell me that it will take some time, and that I should come back in a month.

I begin thinking about how to save up some money for traveling. I ask my friend Adam for advice, and he tells me that I can bake Sudanese bread here in the club, then sell it in front of the embassy. They are always looking for real

Sudanese bread, which cannot be found in any Egyptian restaurants, and I would certainly be able to sell some there.

I like the idea and start baking bread in the club, and hardly has a week gone by before everyone around the embassy knows who I am, and all my bread is sold by noon. I start baking larger quantities, and am able to pull some money together. Only one thing bothers me: One of the embassy workers always insists on taking bread without paying for it, in exchange for which he permits me to sell my goods by the embassy gate. I have no choice but to grudgingly pay this tax.

The issuing of my passport is delayed, and I become quite worried. I ask various friends and acquaintances if they know of any way to speed things up, but to no avail—I have to wait. I continue baking bread and selling it, and continue to save up the money that I will need to travel.

I do not forget my mother, though. With an aching heart, I send her a large amount of money, and wonder whether she will receive it. I have not heard anything from them, and do not know if they are alive and managing to get by. Will the money reach them? I want to stop everything I am doing and head straight back to Wad al-Nar, come what may. Yet I am driven toward an unknown fate, even while the thought of my mother holds me back. And so my heartless body advances toward my fate, while my heart—disembodied— remains at my mother's side.

After the long and agonizing wait—three months and seven days, to be exact—I finally receive my passport. Yet the next question remains unanswered: To which Arab country should I travel? I return to the club and my desperate attempts to obtain a work visa somewhere bear no fruit, for I have neither a degree nor any professional skills. Time passes. I bake my bread and sell it; I keep inquiring after a visa; I pay the bread tax to the embassy worker; and I wait, but no solution comes.

The summer begins and many of the students from the club travel abroad. "Don't you want to go abroad?" Adam asks me. "To Europe, for example?" This idea had never crossed my mind. I had never thought beyond traveling from my village to the capital, but now here I am in Cairo thinking about traveling even farther. Adam's question arouses both hope and fear in me, as well as a certain feeling of strangeness. I laugh and reply, "Europe's no place for someone like me—I don't know a single foreign language. How could I live in a place where I can't understand anyone, and where no one can understand me?"

I do not sleep well that night; I feel lost, and my thoughts are troubled—I begin to seriously consider Adam's suggestion, but I have to wait until the next day to find out more about traveling to Europe.

After a long conversation, after much questioning on my part and much encouragement on Adam's, I make up my mind to travel to Europe, only to encounter another problem with my passport: It is only valid for travel within the Arab world. I go back to the embassy with Adam, where we run into the usual hurdles, but we do not give up until the passport is modified.

Then we go to the French Consulate, which promptly refuses to grant me an entry visa. I return several times, and am refused the visa several times, for many different reasons: once because I am not a student; and once because I am not a businessman; and once they say that it is because I am a foreigner in Egypt, and suggest that I try to get the visa in Sudan. Finally, I go with Adam to one of the tourist offices and pay more than half of the money I have saved to have them arrange for travel to Italy by steamer. Filled with both despair and hope, I can sense myself being driven on by fate toward some new and unknown world.

Adam brings me my passport two weeks later—I have finally obtained the travel visa for Italy. He also brings a friend to lend me some advice, someone who worked in Italy the previous summer. This friend gives me the address of a nightclub where he used to work, as well as the address of some of his friends there.

My departure draws near. Adam comes with me to the port of Alexandria to bid me farewell. He gives me his address, telling me to write him and let him know how I am; and I tell him to write me if anything arrives from my mother.

I check that the amulet is around my neck and Abd al-Malik's watch is on my wrist, and that my bag of palm fronds is hanging across my shoulder. The bag is dear to me; its contents have changed since I left Wad al-Nar, but it itself has remained the same.

Our farewell is warm, quick like the instant between sleeping and wakefulness. The ship moves and the land begins to slide away from me, as I head to yet another unknown world, bearing memories of all that has happened, of the people and the places, while fate lies in wait, readying to load me with new ones.

To Other Cities

As I get off the steamer, I listen to the strange, melodic voices of the people and watch them hug, kiss, and greet one another. All the embracing and kissing taking place in the port seem very strange to me: I have never seen women kiss men—or girls kiss boys—so warmly in public before.

After finishing with the entry procedures, I leave the port and look for the train to Rome. I have no family here, and there is no one waiting to pick me up. I come across a man whose features seem to be Arab and try talking to him. He responds in Arabic, telling me that he too is heading to Rome.

We sit down on one of the station platforms and talk about Italy, and whether there is work to be found here. He tells me that the current situation is not particularly good, and that he has been living here for three years and has worked in several different parts of the country, but has yet to find anything stable.

The train enters the station, and the passengers pick up their belongings and get on. The man and I board together. I realize that I have forgotten to buy a ticket, so I leave him my bag of palm fronds and hurry off the train. I find several windows selling tickets, but I am not sure which one I need, so I pick one at random. Six people are in front of me in line. Every few seconds I anxiously look at my watch—the train will be leaving in five minutes.

Fortunately, the window I chose was the right one. I grab my ticket and hurry back to the train. My acquaintance had told me he would be looking out for me from the window when I return, but I cannot see him. All I see are some people waving to their relatives or saying their goodbyes and chatting in the last few moments before the train's departure.

The man has disappeared without a trace. We were in the blue car, the fourth car of the train—I counted them quickly before going to buy my ticket. I find the car and climb in, but there is still no trace of him. I am overcome with rage as I realize that he has stolen the bag of palm fronds that I had held onto for so long. I turn back and walk through the other cars, peering in all directions like a father looking for his child. The passengers look at me in wonder. I want to ask them if they have seen the man, but I can only speak to them in Arabic.

I am so confused and angry that I fail to notice that a quarter-hour has gone by. I walk back and forth through all the cars, bumping into people and cursing and spitting.

I get off the train and go stand on the platform with my hands on my hips, turning my head in all directions and spitting. I see a man wearing a uniform—he seems to be either the conductor or one of the ticket collectors—and ask him about the car in a mix of Arabic and desperate gestures. He notices that I am holding my passport and ticket in my hand, and takes a look at the ticket, then points to a platform on the opposite end of the station.

I had gone to the wrong track after I had bought my ticket. I hurry over to the other track, but the train has already left the station. I can still make out its caboose, yet soon that too vanishes in the distance. I stand there, angrily cursing my blindness and stupidity, as well as the train that is carrying away my bag.

I sadly sit down on the platform of the station. I have lost the bag that I had held onto throughout my long journey. I have lost a piece of Wad al-Nar, and with it the two dolls I had bought for Halima and Karima at Port Said—I am more upset about those two dolls than I am about losing my clothes.

Thank God I was carrying my passport in a separate, smaller bag that I keep slung across my shoulder. The address in Rome that I had been given is in it, as well as some liras that I had changed earlier.

I go back to the ticket window to try to trade in my ticket, since I had missed the train. After a long linguistic battle—another mix of gestures and speech—I am made to understand that the ticket is also valid on the next train. I ask when that train will arrive, and they tell me ten o'clock that morning.

I leave the station and wander aimlessly about, not knowing what to do. I walk a few steps, then return to the station. I look at the time—it is seven o'clock in the morning. I am hungry but do not feel like eating, so I go outside to a large plaza garden in front of the station and sit there a while. I get up and walk about. I sit down again, still not knowing what to do. I feel like a dog that has lost its master.

Near the entrance to the station, a man is selling grilled potatoes, along with something else that I do not recognize. I buy a bag of potatoes and stand there and eat. He tries to talk to me, but we cannot understand one another. Our languages are different; our lives are different; our concerns are different—everything here is different. For the first time in my life, I know what it truly means to be a stranger. Yet my tongue is tied here, and I cannot even express my feelings to anyone. A sadness takes hold of me: It seems as if every time I travel somewhere new I lose something dear to me.

The train comes. This time I only get on after asking about the destination three times so as not to repeat my mistake. Exhausted, I fall asleep on the train. I want to see this new country, but my physical and psychological state only allows for an angry sleep in which I forget the world.

I wake to the movements of the other passengers. I ask where we are and am made to understand that we have arrived in Rome. I get off the train, the only person not carrying a bag. I am overjoyed when I hear some men speaking Arabic in the station. I ask them about the address I had been given and they explain how to get there, even describing the stores and houses on the various streets so I do not get lost.

I find the street and go to the nightclub that Adam's friend had told me about in Cairo. I find the place closed. I knock on the door but no one opens it. I stop knocking, thinking that I am at the wrong address. I look around for some help, when suddenly a man rubbing his eyes from sleep opens the door. He says something in Italian that I cannot understand and I reply in Arabic, telling him that I have come from Cairo and am looking for someone called Nadir.

He greets me and tells me that he is Nadir, then leads me through a narrow hallway with steps descending underground. The place is dark and cold, and has apparently recently been painted. It looks quite luxurious, and contains many mirrors and multicolored lights. Nadir tells me that he has been working here for two years.

We start up a long conversation about Lebanon, Egypt, and Sudan. He is young, no older than thirty, and comes from Lebanon. He left his country after he lost his house—and with it his wife and young child—in the civil war. Nothing was left for him there, and he wandered all over until chance led him to settle in Rome. In the evenings he works in the nightclub, and during the day he often sleeps there as well. He does rent a small room not far from the club, but most of the time he prefers to simply stay at the nightclub. I ask him what the chances of finding work are, and he replies, "I won't hide it from you, the situation's not very good right now. But you can rest at my place for a day or two until I manage to arrange something for you. Don't worry about anything right now—let's go to my apartment and get something to eat."

On the way I tell him about how I lost my bag. He tells me that I should have asked about it at the station before getting on the train, and that I should have also asked at the station here in Rome—and he promises to check for it later.

We sit down to eat and continue our conversation. We both feel like such strangers here, and it does us good to share our wounds with each other. He has lost his family, his money, and his country. As for me, I do not know if my family is still alive, and there is no part of my country that is not mired in problems—the whole land is being dragged downward by the burden of its people, like an old woman no longer able to support her own weight.

The days go by, but I fail to find any work. In the evenings I spend a few hours at the nightclub where Nadir works and observe this strange new world with him. I see dancing and kissing—this is a place of sex and ecstasy, deprivation and gratification, and also oblivion. I approach this strange world, wanting to experience it, hoping just once to feel some happiness. And so I dance and drink with the women—I wrap my arms around them and kiss them, trying to forget myself. And for a moment I manage to forget it all, even the fact that there is something that I am trying to forget.

Nadir tells me about many things, and I gradually begin to get used to feeling like a stranger here. Indeed, this feeling is what I have come to know best. Nadir manages to find me a job working in the club. During the day I help him carry the cases of drinks into the club, and in the evening I stand at the door and take the men's coats and the women's handbags. I put numbers on them, and give them back to the people when they leave the club.

I enjoy my new job and make a good amount of money in just a short period of time. I begin to pay part of the rent with Nadir—at the beginning he had refused to let me pay anything. We do everything together, and I learn a lot from him on account of his experience and age. He gives me advice whenever I need it, yet I notice that he lives a very stoic existence, not permitting himself any joys or pleasures.

I send my mother a large sum of money and a long letter assuring her that I am doing well. And I tell her that I will soon be coming home.

I begin to learn about Italy, and even get to know a few of the young men and women here. I am pleased with my work and feel like I am slowly settling into this new place, but everything changes when the club's owner arrives. He is blond, about forty-five years old, and has a thin mustache. He has several large rings on his finger, and a bunch of tangled chains hang from his neck. He is very well dressed, and I am told that he also owns a very expensive car called a 'Porsche.' He had been away on summer vacation, and upon his return became quite upset to learn that I was working in the club. I did not know exactly what he was saying; I just heard an argument and the raising of voices. But arguments in any language have a way of being understood.

I was, of course, the cause of this altercation with Nadir. I learned afterward that Nadir had told the owner that they needed someone new to work there, and that his wife—the owner's wife, that is—had agreed to let me have the job. But the owner would not hear any of it, and could not be persuaded otherwise, for under no circumstances would he let a black man from Africa work in his nightclub.

Nadir was almost bursting with rage. I stop working, and Nadir redoubles his efforts to find me a job, but there is nothing to be found. I do not want to be a burden on him, so I ask him if there is any chance of my finding work somewhere else, in another city. He thinks about this for a while, then says, "There's only one good option right now: You should go to France and work in the vineyards. I have a friend there—I'll send a letter with you so he knows to help you out."

Nadir manages to procure me a one-month travel visa to France. This is no easy task, but he knows of certain back channels that facilitate these matters.

I warmly say goodbye to him and wish him well. He presses my hand while speaking to me in his Lebanese dialect, then embraces me. I get on the train to Lyon.

I arrive in Lyon and find Nadir's friend Adham waiting for me at the station. I do not recognize him, but he recognizes me, and greets me, taking my bag. Then we get in his car and head to his place.

He lives in an old house with several other young men. Some of them have jobs, yet several of them are unemployed. All of them, however, welcome me the first day. But the next day, things are less harmonious. They have quite a few arguments, and these get worse throughout the day, subsiding only after nightfall when they all sit down together to play cards.

Four days go by without anyone finding work. I know this is the reason for the edginess and tension, for all their frequent arguments.

The next day a Frenchman comes to the house: he is a short man with a red face, and suspenders fasten his trousers to his enormous belly. He speaks with one of our group, and although I do not understand their conversation I can see my companion's eyes light up with joy. "Let's go," he tells us. "We can work for one week in his fields. He'll pay us, and also give us food and board."

They leave Adham a note telling him where we are. Adham himself works in one of the produce stands at Lyon's Arabic market. He has a steady job with steady pay, and can work the whole year round. He had managed to obtain a legal work permit and so encounters no problems other than the usual prejudices against foreigners, a problem one runs into all over the world.

The four of us get in the man's Peugeot and head to his vineyards. One man from the group—the one the Frenchman had negotiated with—had worked for him a few times in the past. They discuss the specifics of the job in French, then the man takes us to a small wooden house at one of the back corners of the vineyard, a good distance away from the road. The place has three small rooms with bright, clean furnishings, and a fourth room filled with food and drink—the man tells us that all of it is ours, along with everything in the refrigerator. He says we can sleep wherever we want, but that we have to keep the house and all the furniture clean. He will be coming by every afternoon, he says, to check and see how we are working. Finally, he asks us not to go to the village, neither to buy anything nor to contact anyone, so that we do not run into any problems with the police, and so that *he* does not run into any either.

He leaves, and we strip off most of our clothes and set to work. We are allowed to eat as many of the grapes as we want, and instead of finishing the work first and then eating, I get greedy. I eat every other grape I pick until my stomach begins to swell and ache. I often have to stop to gather my strength, but manage to make it through the day. I do not eat with them in the evening. I have diarrhea all night, and the others laugh at my pain and my greed while devouring the contents of the refrigerator like roaches. After the meal they sit around drinking a large bottle of red wine, and follow it up with a bottle of white.

They all get drunk, and one of them stands up and starts singing while another plays the drum and the last one dances. My stomach dances with them in pain, yet I laugh more that night than I have in a long time. Despite the aching in my belly and the relentless diarrhea that keeps dragging me to the bathroom every couple of minutes, I laugh as if I too were drunk.

We fall asleep, exhausted, drunk, and—in my case—in pain. The next day, we sleep in a little, then go to work in the fields. This time I do not put a single grape in my mouth. We work all day, and take breaks to eat something from time to time, before carrying on with the work, which I find quite easy.

In the evening my friends resume the activities of the previous night, but this time I drink with them. The wine tastes completely different from the stuff I used to drink in Omdurman in the days of al-Khattaf and the Whale. I do not want to get drunk and act like they did yesterday, so after a while I leave them and go watch some television. In just a few minutes, however, I fall asleep. I do not wake up until the end of transmission, when I turn off the television and go back to the others, only to find them keeled over in their seats, snoring.

Time passes quickly, and the Frenchman comes by every day to bring us more food, which we greedily devour, and more drinks, which we thirstily gulp down, as if we were storing all of it in our bodies like camels. He pays us at the end of the week and we return to Adham's house. My friends go back to quarreling with one another and playing games of chance, and we all wait for more work.

We remain unemployed for a long time, and I slowly begin to spend the money I had saved up from my job in Italy. I had changed the liras to francs and put them in a bank, as Nadir had advised me. I talk to Adham and tell him that I am worried that the situation will not change. He tells me that he is sorry and that he has a work permit, which means he can work without any trouble. But at the moment, no more permits are being issued to foreigners, and the economic situation here has become so bad that many foreigners have begun returning to their home countries.

My first month in France ends, and with it my legal period of stay. Now, in my second month, I am illegal just like all the rest. I walk the streets like a rat, and whenever I see a police car or an officer's uniform I scurry into the first alley I can find, or rush into a shop at random—I ask for soap at the butcher's and for bread at a bookstore. I have heard about what happens when you get caught: I would be forced to spend the night in prison and would then be deported back to Sudan, while all my money sits in a bank here in France.

My fear and worry grow, and finally I go to the bank and withdraw all my money. Once back at the house, I go to the bathroom so that no one can see me and stitch the money to the inside of my trousers. The others are in dire straits. They have run out of money, and cannot even afford cigarettes anymore.

A few days later, the group decides to go to Holland. They have heard that the situation is better there than in France, and that there is work to be found. I decide to go with them and stick this thing out to the end.

Our main problem is that all our legal periods of stay here in France ended long ago, which means there is no chance of any of us obtaining an entry visa to Holland. But the most experienced man in our group, who has been all over Europe, says he has a way to get us across the border. He suggests that we travel together by train from Lyon to Paris, and from there to Amsterdam via Belgium.

The plan is for all of us to go hide in the train's bathrooms as it approaches the border, and to wait there until the border police have finished going through the train. He says he has traveled this way several times before. As the group listens to him, a look of sudden earnestness appears on their faces. The idea of this dangerous plan scares me, and I try not to show my fear. I look at the others' faces for reassurance, but fail to find any there.

We buy tickets to Paris, and from Paris to Brussels, so that we can stay on the same train until the border. We board the train, and my fear grows with each passing mile. I am drenched in sweat, and begin to wish that I had not undertaken this journey. But the hand of fate keeps pulling me on invisible strings toward danger, toward the unknown. I wish my mother would call me home, save me from this wrenching, wandering existence. I touch the amulet and seek its blessing.

I forget about everything else the moment we split up and head to separate cars of the train. Each of us hides in one of the bathrooms, and the train draws ever closer to the France–Belgium border.

I stay in the bathroom for exactly sixteen minutes, during which I look at my watch more than forty times. I almost come out to give myself up and have them send me away. I hear voices outside, and I know that they have figured out where we are hiding. They are coming after us, taking us out of the bathrooms one after the other. I look for a hole in the door so I can see what is happening, but I cannot find one. So I prick up my ears instead, though I cannot understand a word they are saying. I hold my breath and remain perfectly still.

Time passes, yet the train does not move. I can hear a police car entering the station. I stay nailed to the spot, cursing and swearing to myself. A few more minutes pass, and still I am waiting for the inevitable knock on the bathroom door, for them to take me away, submissive and defeated.

I hear the sound of a police car driving away, and then the train starts up again. I cannot believe that I am still here. I slowly open the bathroom door once the train has picked up some speed, making sure that no one is waiting for me in the corridor. I look for the others but do not find anyone. A little while later, one of them shows up in my car. "Where were you? I've been looking for you," he says.

I reply, "Where are the others? I heard a police car." He lets out a quick laugh and says, "That wasn't the police; it was an ambulance. There was a pregnant woman in your car, and she began going into labor near the border. Fortunately you were wrong about the police."

We look for the others but find no trace of them, and realize that they have been arrested. They have taken away the man who came up with the plan, the one who had traveled all over. I sit down, terrified, and await my fate. Should I continue on to Holland, or stay and hide in Belgium? My companion reassures me once I reveal my uncertainty: The inspection at the border between Belgium and Holland, he says, is not nearly as thorough as the one between Belgium and France.

We hide in the bathrooms once again. There is no trouble this time. We succeed in crossing the border, and arrive in Amsterdam that evening.

We walk through the station and find several people speaking Arabic. We ask them about somewhere to stay, and one of them makes things easy for us by offering us lodging at his place, though for quite a lot of money. We pay it grudgingly, needing some rest after the long journey and the exhausting border inspections. We stay at his place for three days, during which we become acquainted with someone who works in one of the rose farms. He says we can come work with him, and we immediately accept the offer—this is exactly what we had hoped would happen.

The work is enjoyable in the beginning, but after three days my back begins to ache from constantly bending over in the fields. I work long days to save as much money as possible, for the job pays by the hour, and also because I still have a lingering feeling that my stay in this country will soon be coming to an end.

I wear myself out working from seven in the morning to six in the evening. I come back to the house to sleep, and start working again as soon as I wake up. After three weeks of this, I send some more money to my mother in the village, as well as a letter to my friend Adam in Cairo to let him know how I have been managing.

The days go by, each like the one before. Nothing changes. I work like a machine until the sun begins to set, then come back to the house and fall asleep. I do not even have time to think anymore.

The job on the farm comes to an end, and we return to the house of the man we had met at the station and wait for another one. I have saved up a fair amount of money, but it is not enough to pay for a plane ticket to Sudan—I am bent on returning to my village now.

One day I am woken by the sound of bitter crying. Someone else who was living at the house had gone to the bank to withdraw money from his savings account: they told him there were only twenty guilders left in the account. He had saved up a huge sum in order to return to his country and get married. He had been working illegally in Holland for three years, and had worked like a madman to be able to afford a marriage. And now he has been robbed by the closest friend he had in his exile. He met the man in Spain, and they traveled together to Holland and became fast friends. They told each other all their secrets, and once his friend had learned his bank code, he made ready to travel, then went to the bank and emptied out everything in the savings account. He even stole some of his friend's clothes to give them to another housemate of ours, who is now laughing and slapping his hands while this man weeps in his despair.

I curse the thief and try to comfort my suffering companion. But how can you comfort someone who has seen years of labor disappear in an instant, and who knows nothing about the fugitive thief except his name? He does not even know whether all the stories the man had told about himself and his country ever had any truth to them.

I go back to bed and think about the guileful thief. I open up my closet and find my clothes as they were—none of them have been stolen. I look for Abd al-Malik's watch, getting frantic when I cannot find it. He has stolen that as well. I spit on the ground, cursing him again and again, and I curse this house as well. One of my most precious keepsakes—something I had held onto for so long—was gone in an instant, stolen by a brute who cannot even fathom how much it means to me. He will probably throw it away in the first garbage can he passes, or perhaps he will give it to one of his relatives as a gift.

The situation worsens; there is no work to be found anywhere. Autumn sets in, and with it weather colder than anything I have ever felt. I hear stories about icy rain, and about snow that swallows up the streets and covers all the cars and houses. These rumors about the coming winter strike fear in my heart, so I speed up my preparations to leave. I buy a cheap plane ticket back to Egypt—from there I can travel to Sudan by train. I do not have an entry permit for the Netherlands, and I know this is going to cause some problems when I leave, yet I still prepare to head home: Despair has taken hold of me, a deep, irrational despair that drives one to acts that verge on madness.

*

At the airport, I get in the line to go through customs. I feel no fear this time, in spite of the precarious situation I know I am in. I just want to go home. I have been through enough, and seen enough.

The officer opens my passport. He flips through each page looking for the entry visa, but finds nothing. He asks me something in Dutch, and I feign ignorance even though I know what he wants. He calls one of his colleagues over and they inspect my passport together, then the newcomer orders me to follow him to a side room. He asks me several questions, but I only reply in Arabic. I spend four hours there, and they contact an Arabic interpreter who translates as I relate everything that has happened to me. They want me to pay a large fine, but I tell them that all my money is gone. I had changed everything I had into dollars, which I have hidden on the inside of my trousers.

I spend several days in detention, the whole time fearing that they will keep me here until my passport expires, forcing me to buy another one; or that they will search through my pants and take away the money I have worked so hard for. But they finally release me, and allow me to travel to Cairo.

I get on an airplane for the first time in my life, and leave Holland. I feel as if I am the one flying, and not the plane; I feel like a bird that has finally escaped its cage. I think about everything that has happened to me, and cannot shake the loss of my bag and my watch from my mind. The loss of these two keepsakes causes me more pain than the thought of all the time I spent lost in foreign lands.

I surrender to sleep with my hand grasping my amulet, the only thing I have left from Wad al-Nar.

To the Village

I quickly clear customs at the Cairo airport, for there is not much in the small suitcase I am carrying: some clothes, a bracelet I had bought for my mother, and two dolls and some sweets for my sisters.

I go back to the Ain Shams district and ask for Adam, but am told that he has gone to visit his relatives in Sudan. I ask if there are any letters for me, but nothing is there. I stay a day and a half, and everyone is curious about my trip to Europe. I tell the story dozens of times. Some people express amazement, and some of them believe me, but many just laugh and say I am making it all up. It is indeed a strange tale, and so I generally only relate the most credible stuff, and keep the more peculiar parts to myself.

I bid them all farewell and go to the Cairo station to catch the train to the High Dam. The train seems slower this time, but perhaps my anxiousness to see my mother has something to do with this.

As we travel, the signs of life slowly disappear and melt into the earth, until we finally arrive at the High Dam. I go to the old coffeehouse to relive my memories with the frog, drinking something hot this time.

My mind wanders back to the village, and I think of my imminent return while the waiter brings me new cups of tea whenever he pleases.

I hear disturbing news from people traveling in the other direction. They tell me how the famine has spread to even more parts of Sudan, and with it illness and disease. I am worried that something has happened to my mother and sisters—it has been so long since I have heard anything from them. Lost, swallowed up by strange worlds, I had been barred by fate from taking a path of my choosing, and forced to take an unwanted road, not knowing what else to do. But soon the landmarks and the path all disappeared—I had no one, no light to guide me through the dark.

I arrive in Khartoum and pay a quick visit to Omdurman before the next train leaves. I recall the places I lived, and think back to my first days here. A feeling of sorrow and longing overcomes me. The older I get, the more painful my memories seem to become. My childhood is the only source from which I still can draw a touch of happiness. I could almost feel life's meaning as a child, but now all I can feel is death, the slow act of dying.

As the train approaches the village, my heart begins beating violently, so violently that I almost think the other passengers would all hear it if the train were suddenly to stop. The dust rises as the brakes begin to screech, and I see concern on the faces. As for myself, the thought of my homecoming fills me with both joy and fear.

The train comes to a stop. I get off quickly and ask about the car heading to the village that borders mine. I am told that it will leave tomorrow at noon, but I cannot wait that long. I go find the driver and ask him to take me there

86

today, telling him that I am willing to pay ten times the normal price. He agrees, then proceeds to spend a long time looking around for other passengers to come with us. He finds six people, but insists on greedily waiting for more. I beg him once more to get going. He does not get angry, but still refuses to budge.

The car bounces along the sand, heading toward the village. The trip is long and rough. On the way I see some groups of people carrying their belongings on their heads while their children walk beside them. They are leaving their villages.

I am sitting beside the driver, so I ask him about what has been happening here. He tells me things have become much worse in this area, and that the people have no choice but to leave for places that have not yet died. I ask him about Wad al-Nar. He looks at me as if I were crazy, "Do you know anyone there?" he asks.

"My family lives there."

"Haven't you heard the whole place was overrun by disease? Don't you know that everyone's moved to the neighboring villages?"

"When did this happen?"

"At least six months ago."

I lean back in my seat and grab at the air with my hands, then open up the window and spit. The driver asks me several questions, but I only give one-word answers, and he finally leaves me alone.

One year, five months and three days have passed since I left Wad al-Nar. The world has changed. Even I have changed. Nightmarish thoughts invade my mind again. The car advances slowly, and the driver stops once to let the motor rest, and once to relieve himself, and once more to

let the passengers do the same. Everyone in the car is laughing as if nothing had changed, while I soberly sit up front
like someone from another world.

We arrive at the neighboring village. Everything seems even
more austere than it was before. I see one of our neighbors.
She has grown older, and is sitting by herself on the corner
of a small mat. I am not sure that it is her until I am close
enough to look her in the eyes. I impatiently ask her about
Wad al-Nar, and about my mother and sisters. She looks
at me for a moment, then turns her face away, cursing this
world and the next. I ask her again, raising my voice until I
am almost screaming in her face, but to no avail. Something
has clearly broken the woman's mind: Things must be even
worse than I had expected. I hurry on toward my village, but
a familiar voice stops me in my tracks. It is Sheikh al-Faki.
My joy at seeing him is indescribable—people from my village are still alive. But how the young sheikh has aged. He
looks like an old man now. Tears stream from his eyes while
he raises his palms before me and says, "May God keep the
souls of the dead, and those of the living too!"

His benediction ends, but my astonishment does not.
Before I can ask him any questions, he continues in a trem-
bling voice, "Things have gone from bad to worse ever since
you left Wad al-Nar. We'd never seen anything like it, we'd
never even heard of such horrible things, not even in the old
tales. But all lives are in God's hands. Your sister Karima
died first, and then Halima. They both had cholera. But
your mother held on in order to see you; she was hoping
you'd come back soon. We wrote you at the only address
we had, but time drew on, and she finally surrendered to
her fate. She left you her prayers before she died, and asked
God to protect you from evil. She also said that you should

go look for Abd al-Malik's family and live with them, for they're your family now."

The dust kicks up, bringing a long stream of tears to my eyes as Sheikh al-Faki continues, "I buried your mother and the two little ones in the village. The money you sent reached them the first and second time, but they were already with God when the third sum arrived. I still have part of it here for you, and I hope that you'll forgive me for spending the other part."

The dust keeps kicking up into my eyes, and tears keep streaming down my face. I put my hand on his shoulder. "Where's my mother's grave?" I ask him.

"All of Wad al-Nar has become a graveyard," he bitterly replies. "We've been burying eight or ten people every day. Some people have left, but there are others who've stayed, preferring to leave the world in the same place they came into it."

I leave Sheikh al-Faki and continue on my way to Wad al-Nar, with the dust still swirling, the tears still flowing. The village is unrecognizable. I see rubble everywhere, and haphazard piles of stones that mark the graves. The bones of dead animals fill the place. I cannot tell where our house used to stand. Even the old graveyard has vanished, now completely covered by sand. Only one thing remains: the palm tree. My old palm tree. It has toppled over and is lying on its side, half of it visible above the ground, the other half buried in the sand and dirt. I sit down on it and face the ruins of the village.

I take out the two dolls and my mother's bracelet, and dig three graves beside the palm. I bury them there, marking each of them with a large stone that I know will disappear in time. I sit back down on the trunk of the palm and fill the three graves. Then I cry, I weep until the echo of my shrill lamentation fills the place.

And I hear the dead crying with me.

Vienna, 1988